1970

ook may be kept

Mirrors

LUCY WARNER

MIRRORS

stories

Alfred A. Knopf · New York · 1969

THIS IS A BORZOI BOOK

PUBLISHED BY ALFRED A. KNOPF, INC.

First Edition

Library of Congress Catalog Card Number: 69-10697

Manufactured in the United States of America

In memory of W. S. W., Jr.

Contents

Mirrors

How Sweet My Daughter,
How Deep My Anger

The cabinetmaker came again on Saturday. Diplomatic and steady-eyed, he went right to work, leaving Freda and Ned to their quarrel. It was the same every weekend for them: would he please take her and the children to the beach, and on his side, why should he when he disliked public beaches and didn't think they benefited the children. Through the open windows the traffic from Seventh Avenue roared and spit; the windows were all grimy, the cabinetmaker noticed; and the two children were drawing quietly in the corner while no one thought to ask them if they'd like to go to the beach or not. Freda was in tears. She was pointing out what a beautiful day it was, how hot the city, how blue the ocean would be. Her round fresh mouth was quivering. Freda, the cabinetmaker was thinking, had a point.

"Mr. Stone, try to make it level with the top of the window," Freda said to the cabinetmaker in her exasperation.

"I'll do my best."

"Isn't it a perfect day to go to the beach," she asked wistfully.

"That's where I'd be if I weren't here."

"Why *are* you here, by the way?" Ned asked from the corner of the room where he was wrapped up, tangled, and smothering in the *Times*.

"I work in the shop weekdays. Saturday's the only time I get into people's houses."

"That's an odd way of putting it, I must say," said Ned. He had a high, donnish forehead which rose now in a series of perplexed lines.

"Not at all," Freda cried. "Mr. Stone simply means he pays house calls on Saturdays."

"What is he? a doctor?"

The children sprang out from their corner, Nellie in her bare feet, Peter's eyes deeply bored and full of the effort to be otherwise. They poked in the cabinetmaker's black bag.

"Are you a *doctor?*" Nellie called up to him on the stepladder.

"What's your name? *Dr.* Stone! You're no doctor."

"My name's Ivan." He was approaching forty, but accidentally, with no visible signs of age; as though in fact he had forgotten his age.

"What are you building? Can I help?" Peter said, and picked up a hammer; but he was already painfully bored with the hammer.

"I'm building a tall cupboard for your daddy's papers."

"*Daddy's?* Father's you mean."

"Well anyway it'll be tall, tall as a church," Ivan said, realizing this was not an appropriate answer for a twelve-year-old boy.

But Peter said: "Yes," with some interest.

Nellie was toying with the end of Ivan's tape measure. The delicate bones in her feet were relaxed under brown skin; at some point she must have been to the beach. Ivan

4

found himself looking down on the shining top of her head where her pale hair was parted, unevenly, over the crown.

"What's your name and how old are you?"

"Nellie. I'm four years old." She put the tape measure back in the bag as though she had been scolded, but gave Ivan her sulky smile.

"Children, why don't you let Mr. Stone get to work?" said Ned from his corner. It was apparent, suddenly, to Ivan, that this room was the only room in the apartment, except for the children's near the entrance, and the small unlit kitchen. Ned and Freda had no other room in which to hide their anger.

"How can he get to work? The children have no one else to talk to," Freda answered.

"You could take them out. Take them to the park."

"The park's hot and crowded today. Ned, it's a perfect day for the beach."

"They don't bother me," said Ivan. "I'm just measuring up again, like I did last time."

"We weren't home last time," said Peter. "Where are the boards? When are you going to start building?" But it was with tremendous effort that he summoned up these questions.

"I cut the boards in the shop. I believe your father ordered them to be delivered . . ."

"I never ordered any such thing! Freda, you never told me . . ."

"Oh for Christ's sake let's forget the damn cupboard and go to the beach. All of us. You too, Mr. Stone."

"Please call me Ivan."

"Let's just pack up and go! We'll buy hot dogs there, and they have beer at Jones Beach. All of us!" She had stunning red hair and a round betrayed face.

5

"I want to build a cupboard," cried Nellie. But nobody heard, for Ned was storming:

"What? You propose to take a carpenter with us to the beach?"

"Ned, don't be so insulting."

"That's all right, I can't go anyway. No offense." But Ivan swayed on the stepladder. All families were alike in their wretched bickering, yet he always came into them craving for their bliss. The cabinetmaker had a B.A. but somewhere in his mind he associated building things with a simple life and a simple life with families; and somehow he had acquired neither and only wasted an education.

"If the wood hasn't come I'll knock off for the day," he said.

"Oh for God's sake, *I* ordered the boards," Freda said with tears in her eyes, vexed humiliated tears. "I knew Ned would forget. Why don't you come down and have some coffee till they come."

"How can I get any work done with all these people in here? Freda, will you take the children to the park!"

"I will not. They enjoy Mr. Stone's company."

"Please call me Ivan."

"Would this saw cut off a finger?" asked Nellie.

"It would cut off a whole leg," Ivan answered, and could have bitten his tongue. Such a bizarre notion to be giving a child.

He came down from the stepladder apprehensively. Nellie stood with her hair hanging on both sides of her cheeks and her pouted, slightly sulky mouth open a fraction. She had dreamy eyes, like a woman in bed.

"Don't play with that saw," Ivan said, taking it from her.

6

"Come have some coffee. And don't worry about Ned. He wasn't going to work today anyway."

That was true, but only because his favorite chair was off being recaned.

"What sort of work do you do, sir?"

"I'm an economics writer . . ."

"I see."

". . . with liberal tendencies."

"You're not liberal, Father."

"Peter, you don't understand these things. I am decidedly liberal, or we wouldn't be living like a heap of beatniks. Please don't speak up on things you can't follow."

"If you were liberal, Father, you wouldn't mind Ivan's going to the beach with us."

"That's different!" cried Ned in a rage. "I'm speaking of economics."

"It shouldn't be different," Freda said quietly. She looked as though someone had crossed her long ago, and she only spoke in recollection of some better dream.

Just as they were drinking their coffee the wood arrived. Stacked up near the window, the varnished boards made the room even smaller. Constricted, Ned once again demanded that the children be taken to the park. On Freda's refusal, he himself went out, taking the *Times* with him, and not saying good-bye to anyone.

The hot afternoon sun came through the open window like melted butter. With the children beside him, and Freda sewing at the table nearby, Ivan discovered his bliss, shakily, founded on the exclusion of Ned and the re-emergence, temporarily, of Freda's dream. She pulled Nellie to her.

"How sweet my girl is, like an apricot."

"You're very lucky in your children."

7

"Am I? I'm mostly angry at them."

"I haven't seen you angry yet."

"Oh it's all because of them I get angry. I used to be a singer, I was studying opera. My teacher was training me for the Met. In those days I was glorious! I would have sung Isolde by now, but there were the children, and another one on the way you know."

"No. How would I know?" said Ivan in some confusion.

"Mummy's lying. She never sang."

"I'm not lying, Peter darling. I was happy to give up my singing for you and Nellie. But," she said to Ivan, with a change in her voice, as though by this new inflection she could hide from the children what she was saying, "I'll always be angry at the sacrifice."

"You could keep up with your lessons even so," said Ivan, who had stopped drilling into the wall to look at this woman.

"You must be an idiot," Peter was saying, though Ivan wasn't listening. "Are you an idiot? Mummy never sang in her life."

"I'm too old for lessons. At my age one should be on the stage or nothing. Singing in the shower isn't enough."

"Don't listen to her! Don't you see she's crazy?"

"For your own pleasure I meant, you could sing for yourself."

"Sing for myself? When I was nearly ready to sing for the world?" And Freda set aside her sewing and gazed bitterly at Nellie.

"I too had a dream," said Ivan from behind a shaft of sunlight. "I believed I could live simply and raise children, all working together, building and cooking and reading together."

"Yes yes," cried Freda. "I too! How nicely you put it,

how true it used to seem. But haven't you a girl friend?"

"I'm too old myself for such hope."

"Yes, as soon as you are old enough for the hope, you are too old to live by it, that's true, Mr. Stone."

"Please call me Ivan."

"Ivan," she said steadily, "when you are my age you will have forgotten to be sorry."

Ivan went back to drilling, taking the mollies from Nellie's hand as she passed them to him.

"Nellie's going to be a dancer, Ivan," said Peter. "See the way she stands?"

"And you, Peter, what about you?"

"I'm a poet. And I'll tell you something, though you seem too much of a fool to understand it. In this world there is no such thing as a dream unless you live it, and you're not too old for that."

Ivan looked down on this precocious boy with astonishment.

"He always talks like that," laughed Freda. "He gets it from me. It sounds wise from a child and ridiculous from an adult, doesn't it?"

"You're wrong, Peter. All my girl friends want me to get a Ph.D. and a respectable job. That's the end of the dream. I'm too old for simple girls with simple needs, that's the answer to what you said."

"Nellie darling, you're in Ivan's way."

"Not at all. Let her stay."

"I still say you're an idiot to believe Mummy. She never sang in her life."

"But I believe her, Peter. She was telling the truth. Weren't you telling me the truth?" he asked Freda.

And this confrontation collapsed Freda, whose eyes went to pieces under Ivan's. He saw her untidy red hair and the quivering round mouth, her animation given over to a kind of dazed stupidity, and her whole body slack in the chair. With a startled preoccupied voice she said:

"I only wanted to go to the beach today."

The following Saturday the cabinetmaker came to finish the cupboard. Ned stood about approving of it, describing which shelves would do for what, and questioning Ivan on the doors, which remained to be put up.

"Double doors, you say? Sort of French doors, with a latch? And it locks?" He had already dragged out his papers and magazines from a closet and was arranging them in piles on the round oak table where Freda was sewing the hem on Nellie's school skirt.

It was raining and no one mentioned the beach.

Ned's favorite chair was back but the house was too cluttered for him. Nellie sat at his desk drawing, and Peter was sitting on the stepladder in conversation with Ivan. It dawned on Ned, dimly, that Peter, after his usual boredom, took an extraordinary interest in Ivan; for Ivan, as Ned saw him, was a simpleton. With his *Times* under one arm and his briefcase under the other he took himself off to the library.

"I'm just going to spend a few hours working," he said to Freda, giving her, to his own surprise, a kiss on the forehead. Something about Ivan, today, brought out what domesticity Ned had; perhaps because Ivan had, on arrival, so openly admired and played with Nellie.

"You're lucky you have that!" snapped Freda. And Ned was gone.

"He's only nice because of that damn cupboard, and it

was my idea," Freda said huskily, for she was close to tears of agitation. Nellie sat with her hair in her face painfully completing the legs of a man on a stepladder; and Ivan, screwing on the hinges for the doors, glanced occasionally over at her, at the long fall of her hair and the serious pouting profile of her little face. It would seem that Freda was troubled by Ned's kiss which threw out of line her weekend misery.

"Is this any way to live?" she wailed. No one was listening. Ivan and Peter were talking together, while Ivan worked, laboriously, over the bronze hinges.

"Nellie, come over here and try this on," called Freda, brushing threads and pins off the table.

Nellie approached with her diffident sulky manner. She exchanged her blue jeans for the wool skirt reluctantly, scowling at her mother.

"How sweet she is!" Freda said wearily to Ivan.

"Are you finished, Mummy?" cried Nellie. "I want to help Ivan."

"Here, put your jeans back on, darling. And don't bother Ivan."

"Peter's talking to him, so can I."

Nellie put on her jeans and rushed over to Ivan. A sullen girl with lovely restful eyes.

"Nellie!" cried Freda and suddenly broke into quiet tears over the wool skirt; perhaps because the hem was so crooked.

Ivan cut off in the middle of a sentence with Peter to greet Nellie. She flung herself at his waist, her feet rising off the floor, her arms locking at his belt.

"Hello there, sweetheart."

Nellie was in tears. "Will you talk to me too?"

"Of course I'll talk to you, Nellie."

11

"Why does Daddy always go away?"

"He has work to do," said Peter.

But Ivan was uneasy, and unlocked Nellie's arms. It was Saturday, his day for visiting houses, his day for partaking of family joy; he was glad to be left alone with Freda and the children, only everyone seemed to be in tears, except Peter, and Peter was a slim tie between Ivan and the possibilities of family happiness which disintegrated before his eyes. He would hang onto the conversation with Peter though Nellie was crying at his feet. But first he interested Nellie in a leftover flexible bronze hinge. Peter went on talking:

"And what did you do after college?"

"I went to Alaska, with a tent."

"All alone?"

"No." Ivan paused as though to remember precisely. "With a girl. She had red hair. It was summer, little yellow flowers bloomed in the fields like drops of honey. One day we went to the sea, it was pale blue as silk, washing up from Russia. I really believed in Russia then. I believed," he said, meeting Peter's eyes, "in many things then."

"And the girl?" asked Freda from the table where she had flung down Nellie's skirt.

"She missed her pretty dresses. It was an experiment for her, and it failed."

Freda asked him why he hadn't stayed there if he liked it so much.

"I missed the pretty girls," he laughed.

"Don't they have girls in Alaska?" asked Peter.

"I was homesick," Ivan said abruptly.

"I wish the sun were out today," said Freda. "I don't like rain, do you, Ivan?"

"I like weather."

"I like weather too," said Nellie.

"Where did you go after Alaska?" asked Peter on the stepladder from where his often dull now intensely cynical eyes were focused on Ivan's face.

"Don't keep asking him so many questions. Maybe he doesn't want to tell his autobiography."

"I became a carpenter, that's all. Here in the city."

"You did just the right thing," Freda whispered. She and Ivan took a look at each other. He saw himself stand up in her eyes as though he were the product of her own mind; for a moment her illusion of him coincided with his own about himself. He warmed in it. There was a long pause in the room while the rain fell relentlessly outside. Then Peter got off the stepladder, saying:

"I don't believe you ever went to Alaska."

"Look out, Nellie. It's time to put up the doors."

The children cleared out of the way while Ivan set one door up and began to screw in the hinge.

"Oh you've done a beautiful job. What a nice panel that is, in the center."

"I like weather," repeated Nellie.

"You like Ivan too, don't you, pet?" The woman and the daughter looked at Ivan as though they had a thought between them. "What would you think of us all going to the beach in the rain? Would you like that, Peter? Nellie, you'd like that, wouldn't you? And you, Ivan, you could drive us out, Ned didn't take the car. The children would love an afternoon outside with you."

The first door swung on its hinges. Without stopping Ivan picked up the other one.

"I don't think so today," he replied, in perfect accord with some feeling all his own. He preferred it in their house, this modicum of family life. He could not have said why.

A disappointed silence took over the room. Ivan went on working, trying to be mindless of it. Peter, deep in regret, stared out the window at the poking traffic on Seventh Avenue. In the silence Nellie burrowed in her mother's dress, and Freda, with her deceived expression which Ivan briefly noticed, gazed at him solemnly.

The doors were finished and Ivan swung them back and forth a few times too many, for he had nothing to say, and simply swung them.

"It's done."

"There's sawdust inside," said Freda.

"I'll clean that out."

"Oh don't bother. I'll do it."

But Ivan was already inside the huge cupboard.

Nellie laughed and ran toward him; he laughed also with relief to see the little girl come back to life again, and she slammed the doors.

"Hey," called Ivan. "You've locked me in."

It smelled of freshly varnished wood inside. Ivan stood in the small space with the edge of the shelves pressed against his back. He could hear Nellie's soft laugh, and Peter and Freda discussing how to get him out, the whole family standing together outside his beautiful cupboard. He could not remember where the key was, nor could he lift his arms enough to look in his pockets. He listened to their voices. From inside, their voices were the voices of all families, mother and children. And he was at their mercy.

"Keep looking in the bag, Peter. The key might be there."

"I've already looked. Nellie, stop laughing."

"He's in his house," laughed Nellie.

"I don't see how it could have locked by itself. Peter try the lock again."

"*You* try it. I'm looking for the key."

"He's in his house, he's in his house, don't let him out," chanted and laughed Nellie.

Finally Ivan called out. "Peter, you'll have to use the screwdriver. You'll have to pry the doors open." He was surprised at the note of panic in his voice. "Can you do that?"

"If I do it I'll wreck the doors."

"Well you've got to get me out."

Soon Ivan heard close to his waist the sound of wood giving. A crack, a split, and the doors swung back. Stepping out, his hands encountered the shattered wood of his careful work. Peter was scowling up at him.

"Oh that was simply awful!" said Freda. "And now look at the doors. They're chipped, Ivan."

"I'll have to make another set." Ivan was embarrassed in front of them, embarrassed that he had needed them. Belatedly he was frightened. Why, he might have suffocated in there.

"Let's all have some coffee."

Freda and Ivan with coffee, the children with milk, sat at the table, putting their cups down on Ned's papers.

"Were you ever really in Alaska?" asked Peter.

Ivan said nothing.

Freda's eyes turned away from him and gazed into a space as though they would never come back. Yet another family was crossed off for Ivan. He saw her determined, deluded mouth, as though someone had intruded on, and bruised, one more of her possibilities. She would not pull her eyes back to his. Crumpled up in her chair, she shifted until her distraught red hair sheltered her face from Ivan and Peter.

"Why didn't Ivan take us to the beach?" Nellie asked her.

Freda pulled Nellie out of her chair and pressed the little girl against her thigh.

"Oh I only hope the next child is a girl!"

The Minor Repairs of Life

We put the house up for sale again. Large, steep-roofed, white clapboard, peeling under the sills, our house has a broken wooden kitchen step over which Ed trips regularly; the children jump over it; me, I love that broken step, as evidence of the roughness we have endured. The For Sale sign has been kicking around the shed since the last time we put the house on the market, and Ed once again nailed it on the fence by the road. He nailed it up badly—he is not handy with tools—while Neal screamed in protest and Christy took herself upstairs to cry in secret. I was baking a cake, to fill the house with domestic smells and so coax Ed to love us all, and came outside in my apron feeling tears of vexation at seeing Ed clumsily hammering on the sign. If he must do it, must he do it so awkwardly? My father and brother were graceful men; Ed is bearish, with fair hair that topples off his forehead, and thyroid eyes, handsome in his way, with a curled mouth and flat tall cheeks on both sides of his knifish nose. Neal was still screaming: "Daddy, Daddy, we don't want to move!" and I said: "Ed, do you mean it?" remembering how he rolled away from me last night in bed muttering, 'It hasn't been good for me and it hasn't been good for you.' The sign was up, as it had been last month, and I

17

went searching for Christy. But she had vanished, prey to her own worst thoughts.

"If you mean it, Ed, you could have given me more warning."

"What do you need warning for? I've warned you before."

He put his two feet together on the rug and I thought, I'll have to roll up all the rugs. His shoes are worn down irregularly; he looks sad from behind, like a deliveryman. I kissed his bird-in-flight mouth.

"I can't find Christy. She's all upset."

"Rotten place for her to live," Ed pronounced. For all I know he's right. Too many unfurnished rooms for her to hide her wretched little body in. But that's not what he means; he means rotten because he and I live here. But no matter where we live, it will be he and I. Which is something he refuses to reckon with.

I ran across the field to Judy and Jake's. The apple orchard we share has dropped its apples in the long grass; the grass was matted from Neal and Christy and Judy's Paulie and Adam rolling there among the overripe fruit. An Indian summer wind blew me in their kitchen door, into a neat warm room full of their love, Judy's and Jake's. They sat like cats at the table, both slicing apples. Paulie, of an age to kiss, threw himself at me with a kiss, his little red sweater rising to show a fat happy belly.

"Judy," I cried.

"For God's sake, woman, sit down," said Jake, waving the knife and looking at me with his intense amorous eyes.

"Listen, you two, he's put up the sign . . ."

"Take it easy, Alice. He's always doing that."

"This time he means it. You've got to stop him. I will not live in the city again."

"I'll talk to him," said Judy and I knew she would and I knew he'd listen. He's stopped this selling project before, because of her. Judy is beautiful; it's all in the mouth and hair. I love her most when she's most beautiful, for her beauty wins for me the battles with Ed that I must lose, for lack of beauty. And she's always on my side.

"Christy's been in," Jake told me with his meaningful voice. "So we knew the house was for sale again."

"Did she *tell* you?"

"Yes she told us."

"But where is she? I can't find her anywhere."

"She went for a walk."

"Why doesn't she come to *me*?" I cried out.

"Do you like apple pie?" asked Adam from the counter where he was manfully rolling dough around in a storm of flour. " 'Cause if I put salt in it instead of sugar, you'll say NO!"

"Don't spoil my pie," said Judy calmly, and Adam won't.

"Christy was crying," Adam said, with appropriate melancholy over this fact. Adam and Christy will be married in heaven.

The clean pots and pans hanging bottom-up on a board, the fresh little windowpanes glancing out warmly into the field, Paulie with his fat arms around his mother's thigh, all this family serenity gnawed at me who can only create chaos in a similar kitchen with a similar view.

"Well, talk to him, Judy, if you can," I said and went outside. Under the placid twisted apple trees smelling of ripeness and rot.

I know. I've lived there. We had cockroaches like any New York City family, Neal and Christy slept in one room with a view of a shaft, we cooked in the living room, and the traffic from the West Side Highway on raining nights was like the relentless sound of wind in trees. I spoke Spanish with my neighbors, and when the elevator broke down I could walk up nine flights just like anybody else. We will go back there I suppose, to have less space for our anger, our clamoring. Ed will blossom briefly in the activity of the city. I do not romanticize the country, it's hell too; and the house is crumbling under us; there are damp blotches on the ceiling from a leak in the attic; but oh there is space for anger, voices fly off into a summer wind, into the autumn stillness, and Christy has room to stalk off into. And Neal goes from room to room, naming them, Castle, Prison, Water Room, Hotel, and (his favorite) Discomfort Room (the bathroom). As for me, do I want this space so that I can hide from Ed? No. I like the country because there's no escape for him, no zooming subway to take him away. That's me, a sucker. To his big bovine face.

I circled the house, fondly, past the garden where the flowers years ago went to weeds, to take a look at the sign. There it is, the end of my days. For Sale Inquire Within. What will they inquire? Whether it is possible to be happy under a leaking roof? There was Neal, also contemplating the sign. A lanky abrupt little boy with a mind of his own, which usually is my mind. He fights for me like a kitten. We stood together before the sign. It looked peculiarly affixed, as though it really meant it.

"*I* won't talk to them if they come," said Neal.

"Have you seen Christy?"

"No. She ran off."

"Where's Daddy?"

"He's in the Discomfort Room with a book."

"Damn him," I cried. "Taking a shit at a time like this."

Neal and I went through the front door into a burning smell.

"The cake!" he howled joyfully but with anguish. See what I mean, I create a kind of chaos all the time. Having deprived the children of a good dessert, I raged into the kitchen.

"And it's all Ed's damn fault," I screamed.

"Ed doesn't care," said Christy; she was sitting on the stool, calmly, all her tears shed elsewhere. I took out the burnt cake hesitatingly, hesitant before the deeper sufferings of my daughter. "He doesn't care if we die," she said slowly. "Do you?"

I hugged Christy. Her head, because she was on the tall stool, came to my shoulder. Such a sour beaten little girl, barely seven, with eyes like olives and her father's fair thin hair; she has an unusually triangular face for a child and a serenely mournful mouth; she takes all my sorrows into her face.

"Christy sweet, maybe we won't have to move."

"Oh yes we will."

"Do you mind so much if we do? Don't you remember our nice apartment? Remember how I used to push you in the supermarket wagon? Remember the Number Five bus on Riverside Drive?"

"I remember."

"It was a drag," said Neal, poking hopefully into the cake. "And I'll have to learn how to use a knife."

"Whatever do you mean?"

"All the kids in school there have switchblades. You know that, Mommy."

"That's crazy! Ed!" I went screaming upstairs. "Do you hear this child, do you want Neal with a switchblade in

21

his pocket?" Total silence. "Ed! If you take this boy back to the city, if you *think* you can do a thing like that, I'll stay here with the children and you can take down your damn sign this minute."

Through the bathroom door came his undisturbed voice: "Don't be a fool, Alice." He came out holding *Herzog* in his hand; years later he catches up on the best sellers. He turned his bugging eyes onto my face which burned under his steady pierce.

"Ed, haven't we been happy here? Remember in the spring when the apple trees were in bloom? Do you realize what you're doing?"

"I'm packing us out of this godforsaken place, that's what I'm doing. Out of this foul rotten house where my children are rotting like the whole house is rotting."

"How can you say that, when the children are miserable about the sign?"

"They'll forget soon enough."

"You're breaking their hearts."

"You're not breaking mine," he said, and went into the bedroom.

"Mommy, here's Judy," Neal was calling.

I went down. Judy sat in the living room on the shabby sofa. Why is everything so shabby? The same shabby furniture will accompany us to the city.

"Judy, thank God you've come. Will you talk to Ed? This is all crazy, Neal's planning to buy a switchblade . . ."

"I'll have to, Mommy."

"Ed will buy it," said my scornful daughter, little knowing.

"Oh, he'll come round," said Judy. "And by the way, I think you have some prospective buyers so you'd better decide quickly. There's a couple outside looking the house over."

"Neal," I said quietly, with a fear like a lump in my gut. "Go get your father, will you."

Christy and I went to the window and looked out into the serene afternoon. A young man and woman were standing together with their happiness in their faces considering the possibility of shared joy under this steep roof. I heard Ed coming down the stairs behind us, quickly, in expectation. We've had prospective buyers before, whenever the sign went up, but the sign always came down; this time, I felt, time was running out.

"Ask them in," said Ed.

Shyly, cautiously, as though by my caution to fend them off, I opened the door, Christy hovering beside me.

"Please Daddy, don't," she said in the smallest possible voice.

Over my shoulder I heard Judy speaking up in confidence, the assurance that beauty has:

"Ed, I wonder if you've thought this over enough, for Alice and the children—"

"Ask them in," barked Ed.

I confronted the two young people across a stretch of uncut grass. They came forward without hesitation, an earnest young man with boyish charm beside his pretty little wife. Did Ed and I look like this when we came for the house? But I am not pretty and Ed is not earnest; yet we came with such expectant faces. We were, more or less, happy in those days.

"We saw your sign," said the young man.

"It's a sweet house," she said.

"Our name is French," he said, as though explaining a deep riddle.

"Please come in."

Christy dove back, her hair swinging over her face, and I heard her small voice drop her last words again: "Please Daddy, don't." Then she rushed upstairs.

"My husband, Judy El Greco, the Frenches," I said as though we were all at a party. We sat down.

"Such a sweet house," said Mrs. French.

"It needs a lot of repairs," I said.

"Minor ones," Ed added.

"And this is my son Neal."

"Hello there, son."

"Are you buying our house?" he asked, aghast.

"We'd like to look it over," Mrs. French said, smiling sweetly.

Decidedly they would be happy here. They looked well together. With his hand over hers he asked to be shown around. Neal refused to budge from his chair and stared balefully at them. Judy was looking with all her beauty in her face glowing toward Ed, who was not looking back, so I got up and took them into the kitchen.

"What the hell happened in here?" barked Ed.

"I burnt the cake," I said timidly, and showed Mrs. French the stove and the icebox. The icebox was jammed with food and I shut the door quickly.

"Have you any definite time in mind for moving in?" asked Ed.

"Oh we'd like to move in as soon as possible."

The deeper hopes, the reluctance to give up the dream. We might have been happy here. The dream since I was an adolescent to live in a house. My son and daughter, dream children. To be replaced by this adorable couple, the Frenches, to have my house taken away into the hands of less-equipped dreamers. We came, Ed and I, with our

24

loaded trunks, with our sleepy children. But Christy's eyes were wide with pleasure above her yawns. We came one foggy New England evening and saw our house beside the orchard. We all together claimed it; Neal said sleepily The Farm. White with its small-paned windows obscurely blank promising everything behind the fog, the high-pitched roof sheltering the empty rooms, all my dream, brought up from childhood, from the days spent in just such a house with my parents, the wish to repeat, to own, to belong, this is my house.

"We're eager to move out as soon as possible," said Ed.

I took the Frenches upstairs into the innumerable rooms under the eaves, followed by Ed, Judy, and Neal. In one room we came across Christy curled up in a chair. She gave us her grieved, deprived look.

"Hello there," said Mrs. French.

Two round squeezed tears rested on Christy's cheeks.

"She doesn't want to leave," I explained hopefully; perhaps to spare my daughter they would not take the house.

"I don't care," said Christy.

"*I* care," said Neal. "And Mommy doesn't want to leave either."

"Have you another house in mind?" asked Mrs. French, turning her vapid pretty face to Ed. It was competition to Judy, and Judy knew it.

"We're going back to New York."

"They're not even sure," said Judy. We all sat down around the sorrowing Christy. "You see," she said, watching Ed, "they haven't really decided to move."

"Oh?" said Mrs. French.

"Of course we have, Judy," spoke up Ed. "It's all settled."

"The country is a terrible place to live," Judy went on

bravely, for it was a lie to her and she is a truthful woman. "Terrible. I know. We live right next door. So hard to get your friends to visit." Lie after lie, as their house is full every weekend.

"We're used to the country. We've always lived in the country," said Mr. French, speaking for the first time in a long time. "Are you really so sorry to leave?" he asked me, and his charming eyes pretended to be reflecting some charm he found in my face.

"Very sorry, awfully . . ." I confessed quietly, for his eyes induced confidences. If I had any charm I would have turned it on.

"And how about you, son," he asked Neal. "You're sorry too?"

"Daddy says it's time to migrate, whatever that means." He is suspicious of charm, having been exposed to so little of it.

"Not all animals migrate you must remember, some just dig in," said Mr. French. "And even those who do, like the salmon, don't migrate every year."

"Is that true?" asked Neal with a flush of interest.

"We've been here more than a year," said Ed. "It's time to move. I belong in the city. I prefer it."

"Do you have any difficulty with the house, the heating or anything like that?" asked Mrs. French; she was persistent in her desire to drive us out.

"It's cold," said Christy, whose arms were wrapped around her little rib cage; two more perfectly round tears had collected on her cheeks; her mouth, slightly open, quivered from the cold or from the tears, and she fixed her eyes on Mr. French with a kind of hope I could well understand.

"There are too many rooms," said Neal. "The Water Room where the leak is, The Castle . . ."

"That's enough," Ed said.

". . . and the Discomfort Room, where there's no heat," he persisted gleefully; he had caught onto Mrs. French's needs quickly, more quickly than I had. She wanted comforts, she would not find them here.

"The windows rattle," I cried happily, inspired by Neal who gave me his most conspiratorial, adoring look; we were in it together now.

"All the heat rises up to these top rooms which you can't use because they're so damp, from the leaks you know," I went on.

"You can't fix up a house like this," said Judy. "The beams are probably rotted, the sills and such. Jake, that's my husband, explained it all to me. Our house isn't so old, you see, we haven't got a leak."

"Your heat's great," said Neal, putting envy into his voice. "I bet it's warm in the morning, isn't it, Judy?"

"Very!"

"I hate to get up in the morning, it's so cold," Neal said.

"On your feet," said Christy, "the bottoms of my feet."

Oh my blessed children. I was speechless with joy. Mrs. French looked very cold herself and seemed to be contemplating some inner vision of comfort to be found elsewhere. Then I looked again at Mr. French.

"You've had a very hard life here, then?" he asked, and I was trapped. If I told them that one could be happy in spite of the cold, then Mrs. French would want to find her happiness here. I denied my love for the house:

"Yes," I said, to Ed's and Neal's surprise; they expected

the truth from me, but I saw that the way to win my house was to lie. "It's very hard living here when so much is against you."

"Alice!"

"But you have very staunch children," said Mr. French as though he understood everything.

"We don't stink," protested Neal.

"Staunch, not stench," Ed said; he was aghast.

"What does that mean?"

"You'll stick up for your mother," explained Mr. French. "You're a fine boy."

"We don't want to leave," said Neal in a suddenly forthright voice, like a beg.

"Neal!" snapped Ed. "This is nonsense. It's all decided. We're moving out as soon as possible, as soon as we have a buyer. Are you or are you not interested?" he asked Mrs. French, whose dwindling hopes had still left a little courage in her face.

"Well it's a sweet house. I've always wanted to live in an old house. Dear, haven't I always said I wanted to live in an old house?"

"Yes," he said, "you have."

"But that's the point," said Judy. "These old houses are museums. They're cold and impractical. They're not fit to live in."

But Ed wasn't listening; he seemed to be considering something new and he looked feverishly at me. "This house is for sale."

"But you've been happy here nonetheless, haven't you?" asked Mr. French and his charming blue eyes, blue like sweet little saucers, again reflected some charm he found in my face.

"Yes very," I admitted, knowing I was losing. I was

more bowled over by my need for his sympathy than by my need to keep the house, even by lies; this surprised me. I felt for the first time in years that I had a face and a life. "It's a beautiful house, a beautiful house, when the fog comes in we're so snug inside, the small windows you see, they make you so snug, and in the summer when the wind blows through whistling in the screens, and look at the view, look, right into that dipping little field and the orchard, we pick our own apples, and in the wintertime we light the fires downstairs and it's very warm then. It's a beautiful house, a very beautiful house. I've been very happy here."

Mr. French nodded.

"Mommy," said Neal. Ed was still staring at me. Why? when I'd just sold his house for him. In an agony of confession I went on, with the children's eyes glued to my treacherous face:

"If it's cold, it's nice that way, you run downstairs into the kitchen where it's warm, you light the stove and sit up close to it, the children love that, they run down in the morning and put their bare feet up against the stove. It's a beautiful house, it makes you feel at home. Did you see the way it sits on the grass, it's all settled down like an old person, like an old cat all comfortable . . ." Suddenly I felt the tears and looked at Christy. "I'm sorry, baby," I said, and she nodded, the little tears still on her cheeks. I had betrayed them both for Mr. French's sympathy. There was, I suppose, an awkward silence in the room, but I was obscurely happy.

"Oh it sounds perfectly lovely," said Mrs. French, all her hopes resurrected now.

"Yes it does," said her husband. "Lovely. But very much as though you really haven't decided to sell it, am I right?"

Ed had been speechless for so long that I looked askance at him. I saw his big angry face from a great distance, as though, having confessed myself, I will never be recognized again.

"No!" he bellowed in the small cold room. "No! We are not selling this house. Neal, go take down the sign before someone else comes. Go on!" he bellowed as Neal sat ramrod straight with a stunned mouth and terribly, deeply confused eyes. "Go!" Neal ran out. "We are not selling this house," he repeated in a controlled definite voice.

"Well we're awfully sorry," said Mrs. French in some confusion. "It *did* sound perfect."

"Sorry to have taken up your time," said Mr. French.

We all went downstairs, Christy running ahead, and I saw through the hall window Neal hauling the sign off to the shed in puzzled haste.

"Sorry to have misled you," said Ed without the slightest tone of regret. He shook both their hands and the two of them went out the door, she with some amazement, and he not without saying to me gently: "I do hope you'll go on being very happy here."

I said nothing to the stranger beside me who is my husband. Judy went away without a word, her beauty for once having failed her. We waited until Christy, in an agony of joy, went flying out the kitchen door.

"Well Ed . . ."

"Damn you! Do you think I'd let a pair of fools like that have this house? A sly bastard like that, flirting with you, coaxing you. Wheedling damn bastard!"

"He wasn't flirting."

"Taking advantage of your stupid sentimentality. I'd give him this house in hell. We'll give them a few days

to find a place, and put up the sign again. I won't have anyone prying into my wife's life. I thought you'd outgrown
those kinds of tactics. I misjudged you, as usual."

And he stormed upstairs.

Silence in the big damp house. I went into the kitchen
and inspected the burnt cake, considering making another
try. We are, temporarily, Neal, Christy, and myself, rescued and made safe. But I know I will never be happy here
again; what is a dream compared to a pair of eyes that see
your face.

Out the kitchen window I see my ecstatic daughter
Christy flying in the orchard, running to meet Adam. They
grip each other's arms and tumble in the long grass like
seals. Serene afternoon swirls in the sky. And my unac-
customed heart lunges in my chest. Many long hard days
will pass under this roof.

A Born Homemaker

All the time they bombarded me with their lives. Then I saw myself reflected in kitchen knives, or through the silver-topped bottles in a bar mirror: surprised: hey that's Minna, that's me. And those of my friends who lived or else lived and let live; who made a life of the East Village and called me civilized, who published books and called me an amateur, who ran off to South Africa with a jazz musician and called me careful, who hustled and called me rich, or else who lived on Madison Avenue and called me "interesting" —they handed me a definition like a gift and left me obliged and tentative: a traveler in their city. The cement of their city knocks my footsteps back up into the knee: no resiliency there, not the soft stride on grass to which I am accustomed. Underground, the swaying subway rocks me like a mother. There is a cliff on every street corner where small buildings make small openings. I skirt the cliff and go round the block under the discreet fatherly height of West Village houses. And then I see myself reflected in a window looking out at me from the gloom, the sun just missing the window and keeping me in the gloom, and we take a look at each other in passing.

So little do we find out about ourselves from our friends and neighbors.

Everyone has a story and so have I. And everyone thinks his story is essentially interesting to himself and a bit dull to others. Friends, let me tell you something; the sun is shining and perhaps I am no different from you. Perhaps what you named me was me every time. For I have seen myself in too many returning surfaces, concave, convex, shattered and given back like a broken jug, and face to face but reversed. I never could tell right from left, from looking in mirrors too often where the left hand raised greets the right hand in the glass. Even in friends' eyes I see a small reversed me like a design in a marble. And there are stranger moments than that. Remember the day we saw a woman drop a loaf of bread in a puddle? We had a good laugh over that one, and so did she; she saw the comic side very quickly, considering. And then I felt your mouth on my face laughing away. And that was worse than seeing myself reflected in the puddle. And all of a sudden we scattered; the woman left the soggy bread in the mud and you went away across the street, and I turned corners relentlessly, your mouth still operating on my face. Moments like that can scare you for a day. And my whole life has been made up of such moments.

I came out of puberty fat, and shy as a pony; for my mother, who disliked hair, had mine cut manelike on my head. I was eager to please and the little boys spotted that. So did old men, and the gardener on my uncle's grounds—yes there's money in my family—caught onto my willingness and made love at me fully dressed on some very uncomfortable undergrowth in the woods. He must have guessed I wouldn't tell my uncle and I didn't but he

was fired anyway: obscenely caught on his hands and
knees in the shed with my uncle's big dog. Must have
been a difficult confrontation for my uncle. He wears pat-
ent leather slippers and a smoking jacket and only men-
tions sex when he's referring to the gender of an animal.
I spent a lot of time in my early adolescence at my uncle's, for there were things going on under my mother's
roof that would have been distracting for a little girl. My
mother was a widow and blossomed in her black weeds.
So I spent summers and vacations at my uncle's, and
found there were things going on under any roof, or in
any woods so to speak. My initiation wasn't bad; I hung
around waiting for the gardener but he was haughty after
that and ignored me. And then he was fired. Traumatic
moment for a nymphette who had caused momentary
nympholepsy in a gardener. I walked in the woods in late
summer and felt that my past had been pillaged, that
there was no evidence visible among the trees of joy or
crime; perhaps I had made it up. It was the first difficult
moment of my life.

So then I wanted to go home to my mother and home I
went. To years of Puritanism. My mother made it look
as though her gentlemen callers were there to entertain
me, and so they did. That is, they chattered with me
about school and took me to museums and bought me
edifying books—the classics—to fill in my education.
And sometimes they looked at me as though the gardener's handprints were stamped on my skin, but they didn't
make passes at me; and late at night they made up to my
mother for the daylight hours which they had spent with
me. Which frankly shocked me. I renounced sex forever
and one day I told my mother what the gardener had
done to me and she shed tears of pity and shame and I

shed tears of relief. And somewhere along the line without noticing its disappearance I had lost my willingness. I became stubborn as a mule and this disturbed my boyfriends, for I believe I looked fat and sexy. What I wanted my boyfriends to do was buy me sodas and take me to the movies, preferably in a car, and hands off. But nonetheless I counted on their return attempts, was eager for the picture of myself in their eyes.

My schooling was finished one rainy day in June, with white flowers pinned on my front and the fading spots of measles on my face. In the yearbook I was predicted to be a "born homemaker." Now where did they ever get that idea? I spent the summer studying typing and shorthand and then I struck out. My mother shed tears then too, sent on to me in my apartment in New York curtains, a bedspread, and pillows. I found myself a job effortlessly, in a large magazine office where I typed and filed letters, sealed and stamped letters, mailed them to their rightful receivers. I was still a round young person bursting from my skirts and with an accompanyingly round anxious face: little mother to all the world. Would cook you supper any night of the week. Wear my most uncomfortable high-heel shoes and walk blocks with you while you poured out your soul, such as it was. Look pretty for your vanity and be solicitous for your soul, but go to bed with you I would not. Which made you beg at my door. Men are nicest then, though a trifle hangdog about the mouth. But this could not last forever; fat people have an unerring need for comfort, flee from it though they may. Came along such a nice graceful gentleman, a publisher with respectability stinking from every pore, who put it right on the line: he'd pay my rent and take me shopping, would make so few demands on the rest of my life; I could go out with the boys provided I was home when he wanted me to be, which meant when his wife would let him out. She let him out frequently. Now what would my mother have said to a proposal like that? Go ahead, she'd have said. So I did. He was such a nice, ponderous man, bearing his briefcase like a soldier his pack. He suggested I go on a diet; I lost twenty pounds and was taken to Bendel's and dressed chicly. I still have those clothes, though they have frayed in the interval. Years went by happily. I typed letters at work and mailed them, and was home when asked to be, dressed up for an occasional play or concert or restaurant where we received the I-can-see-what-you-are treatment. Well, a middle-aged man, balding, serious, officious, deferential, cozy, with a slendering late teen-ager in her coiffed hair holding his sweaty hand while we drank champagne: could anyone have taken us for father and daughter?

With no rent or clothes money to shell out, I saved quite a lot, though my publisher, fearing the worst, kept telling me to quit my job. Instead I acquired several sex-less young men. I was no longer fat and no one could have thought me willing; no, they thought me rich and tender-hearted. Sad young men, sleeping all day, high all night, mainlining, painting, living in a sexy high where sex was a hard stone in the gut, jobless, sad oh so sad. I gave them money just to have their time, to spend an early evening with them, to wake them from a shallow sleep and walk in the park with them in the autumn skies—my best friends. I cooked meals for them and bought them sweaters for winter and when they passed suddenly out of my life I took on their friends. I knew nothing about painting or politics or drugs; I was their respectable and rich friend, well set up, their temporary escape route.

Also I made friends with my uptown co-workers, smart young women who'd been to college and told me so, but thought I was bizarre and daring. So I ask you, where did I belong? At ease in the Madison Avenue apartment of a female editorial assistant sipping Dubonnet, at ease walking in the park with a painter on a Sunday afternoon drawing nudes on the pavement and whistling in the wind all the songs we ever knew. I shifted gears as easily as a well-oiled, standard shift car; on the nights when I was sipping my Dubonnet on Madison Avenue and talking casually about Faulkner, the picture would crop up in my mind that tomorrow I'd be strolling out with a jobless boy who had just shot up heroin and would hold me by the arm like a brother and take all my cash in the evening.

As for my publisher he one day let himself into my apartment unannounced and found me in bed with Ivan. Well that was all: in the bed. Poor boy was cold and tired, hungry, with pink-cold ears and nose. I had bundled him under the covers and got in myself to comfort him, which is where my publisher found us and why he cut off funds and his acquaintance with me. I haven't seen him to this day. And Ivan was crushed, for me. He begged my forgiveness, said he'd ruined my life, cried, banged around beating his head with his palms, and finally burst out into a laugh: Minna, my love he cried, you're one of us now. We romped around hugging and crying. We ate up all the leftover expensive food we would ever see again and polished off the last bottle of good liquor. I put on my best dress and we went out into the streets and while there was some cash left we bought him a long warm scarf; and we found a bar where we spent the last pocket money on champagne and shrimps—and then I was one of them. No money left and none coming in except my small pay check which would just cover my rent but wouldn't stretch to cover Ivan. So Ivan and I closed out my apartment and moved my things to his in the East Village, and there I lived for two years. And not once did we make love. He was in no shape to, poor lad. Perhaps he did with the boys, for he liked them best. But he always came home and I was never lonely. He slept next to me like a cat and I washed his clothes and ironed his shirts and when he was coming down from a high and weeping with the surprise I held his head and rocked him like a child. One day he vanished without taking his scarf. But it was summer, and perhaps by then he'd bedded down, raw-lunged, sweaty, weeping, but warm.

Ivan bequeathed to me a fourteen-year-old runaway, Danny, he'd taken in from Forty-second Street. A cheeky boy, strapped into his pants so tight he could barely walk, who came and went from the apartment depending on what he had better to do. He was very attractive to older men; one day he bragged of this publisher, rich as Croesus, yes indeed, my old publisher finding out what he should have been all along. Danny came home to me when he was out on his ear and he nuzzled into bed with me.

Strike out. Twenty-four and what behind me: a gardener, a would-be faggot of a publisher, the sexless boys I had supported, Ivan sleeping sweetly at my side, Danny like a baby suckling pig. At home from one end of Manhattan to the other. If I had money it went for Danny's heroin: my best friend, my child, my love Danny crawling out of the subways onto the street into the last light of day, coming home to me ditched at dawn, crying small

38

boy Danny: a kid. Good clothes can go a long way: I still frequented Madison Avenue, had my respectable friends, the college girls, my job. Home every night with a hope for Danny's arrival. One night when he didn't arrive: me yelling drunk screaming for Ivan long gone, I found his tee shirt in the back of the closet, broke every plate in the house screeching: Irish cop called in by a neighbor. Decent Irish cop: you've had one too many, he said, with Irish appreciation; have a cup of coffee he said and we had one together. Phone shut off; couldn't pay the bill. A nervous gracious young poet just published a book: his cold hands, fingers that turned up on the ends, told me my mouth was grim. Summer spent breathless, the dark corners of bars, no one goes to the beach here, let the sun shine all by itself. Trees thick in the Squares, the head thick from a night of Danny and wine, the fans in subways turning hot air back on itself, eyes avoiding sunlight. Daydream of the ocean, a true daydream from the past, myself a child hand-in-hand with a father walking in the sand, grit of sandwiches with sand on the chicken, Cokes gone lukewarm in the sun: once brown in the summer—once. Now summer runs out dies in the bar a shabby death. Danny's been to Southampton, see his brown chest. Money to spend: a steak, champagne. Danny brags about his connections: if I ever want a place on the beach he'll fix it up for me. On the beach? We drink and nestle like a mother with a feeding child. Dawn; Danny gone, leaving his Coppertone Suntan Lotion on the sink. Can't go back to work; too many years of sending letters to other people, had begun to address them to myself. "Dear Professor Fitzhugh-Greene, We are hoping to have a piece from you, about 15,000 words, by . . . Yours of

Sept. 12 referred to . . ." Mailed to my house. Fired at last. Out on my ear. The surreptitious curiosity of my college-girl co-workers: fired.

Danny I say I need cash fast. From the blue he produces heroin. Nights on the walk, selling it, nosing out cops, plenty of money but the frantic hands on my door. Danny I say this isn't for me, get me out. Then get out he says, but watch it. New York Telephone Company still wants its money but I drop the apartment and move west. To the small trim houses of the West Village. Danny vanished. The cold-fingered poet searches me out every few weeks. My mother comes through with three hundred dollars and a word for the wise. A friend Judith marches on Washington and one day leaves for Africa with a jazz musician, writes me about the free life. Sure. Skies big over land, clouds coming up from the west, wind hodgepodge in the trees. But where is that? I take my three hundred dollars and buy a bookcase, a table, two blue chairs—I'm partial to blue—and civilize myself. How do you suppose Professor Fitzhugh-Greene is doing. I'm broke. Comb the streets for Danny and who do I find instead? Ivan. Ivan. Gone all the way. Fastidious, pretty, my boy Ivan. No more long woolly scarves for Ivan. Stark daylight; we shake hands, his voice pitched high, sleek eyes. Oh Ivan I cry. Minna he says how are you? Oh Ivan I cry. Making do? he asks. Oh Ivan. You're looking just marvelous Minna. Oh. Ivan. I cry.

Call my college-girl friends. Why *hello* they chirp, where are you working now? Do come by for a drink, *love* to see you. I turn up, bleary-eyed, full of tales, lies, how I'm engaged to a poet; their eyes enlarge: How *sweet*. Turned out before midnight; they go to bed early on Madison Avenue. I go looking for the poet with the cold hands; where have you been, he went to Spain last week. True: where have I been? All I know is that I'm pregnant with his child. By all laws it has to be his child. I know what to do in this situation; but in the mirror my own face looks back and that shouldn't be so.

Money gone, I baby-sit for other women's children, receive their kisses in the crisp December wind. We walk to little parks and they swing in the sun, my hands on their bundled coats, pushing them up into the sky: Whee! they cry. They jump off and romp at me with fresh cheeks. One boy—little boy of all mothers' hearts—in a sailor suit: Jimmie. Jimmie and I buy apples in the Italian markets, Jimmie spends his mother's money, we eat the apples in the sunlight. The blood rushes in my skin, I kiss Jimmie on the mouth. Ugh! he says and we laugh. But Jimmie I love you. I love you too you're much more fun than Mummy but I don't like *kissing*. Someday you will. Ugh! he says again and we laugh and I kiss him on the mouth once more. Ugh! he says, if you do that again I'll bite you. I do it again. He bites me. We laugh. His hands in mittens. A muffler around his throat. I kiss him at the base of the neck, under the wool. Ugh! he says. The next morning he throws his arms around me and kisses me on the mouth in front of his mother. Jimmie! I say. Minna I love you he says in front of his mother. He kisses me again on the mouth and my mouth sticks on his. His mother says he has a cold and has to stay home today with the cleaning lady. I don't have a cold says Jimmie. Yes you have she says. And I'm fired.

I had a father, an ordinary man. Committed suicide in a financial slump. I was his baby daughter. I clung to him, rode on his hip like a monkey. Odd that he should give me up for dying. When I stole by Jimmie's house one cold day near Christmas I saw Jimmie through the window in a warm room throwing spirals of rope into the air. Jimmie! I thought. I'd have frozen to death on the spot for that kid. Though I'm sordid to the bone, kissing little boys on the mouth. That December day I stood and saw wreaths at the mantelpiece, a string of holly, red berries for Mary, Jesus coming in at rush hour: Jimmie. Forgive me my perverseness; I loved your little mittened hands, your two blunt eyes. My father was an ordinary man.

It was just before Christmas. Jimmie would wake up to Santa. I could not find Danny, did not want to find Ivan. I had crossed off my mother for holidays long ago. And my uncle. But he wrote, as he always did at Christmas, Dear Minna, it's been so long . . . love to have you over the holidays. This time, okay, I'll go. I called him, collect, from a phone booth: I'm broke, sorry to reverse charges, how are you? Minna my dear girl, let me wire you train fare. I received the money, I bought a ticket, I rode the train into the countryside with my leftover best clothes in the suitcase and my face plastered with make-up to cover the tired years. Trees flicked by, snow deep under their limbs; water wobbly with wind; fences bare in the light. Sun aslant on the hills; houses restrained behind curtains, glancing comfortably into snowy fields. The chill stations, breath ballooning from conductors, the hugs of passengers and greeters. Darkness over the earth, the cigarette smoke in the smoking car layering up on the windows, a refugee look on the faces of people who wished they had gotten off the train in daylight. Myself included. Finally my stop; the conductor in his frayed uniform and gray distinguished face lifts my suitcase down onto the platform; the strike of bitter cold air. My uncle looking manfully among the passengers: Minna! Yes it's me. Cold cheek against cold cheek, avuncular kiss. Bracelets of cold on wrists and ankles, the face smacked with air. We drive into the night, the heater discharging blocks of warmth. His large stately house behind the hedges, the thud of the front door, deep rugs under frozen feet, the discreet shine of polished silver boxes on tables, sheen of mahogany chairs, a fire resting in the grate, the tall leather height of books in their shelves, hot whiskey in a glass cup with a glass handle. My uncle. I weep at his side. Minna! he says. Just tired I cry. We'll send you right off to bed he says, and off I go. Up stairs red with carpets into linen sheets, and the curtains thick against the dark. The bed where I used to sleep. I felt my face go twelve years old under my skin.

In the morning I go down to eggs on a covered dish served by the maid, toast in a silver rack, the coffee hot in its pitcher. Minna my dear, says my uncle, I've been thoughtless, living alone, I haven't given you enough consideration, why don't you stay with me a few months, you're not working are you? NO! Stay here and we'll make some small financial arrangement for the future. NO I want to go back. But you'll stay for Christmas? YES but then I'll go back. So I'm in tears over the eggs. But Minna you're not looking well. I'm not feeling well I cry. If you stay here I could introduce you to a very nice young man he laughs. Not for me, I have plenty of nice young men I cry. Have you? well, I'm glad to hear it, one day you'll settle down and I'll come to the wedding. Not me no wedding for me, that's not the kind of nice young men I know I cry. No? well times have changed, when I married your aunt weddings were all the rage. Not any more I cry.

Christmas came and went as Christmases come and go. I stole some money from my uncle's wallet and bought him a scarf which pleased him very much and he bought me a book, a long bathrobe, a pair of classy gloves, and some lemon soap. He drove me to the station before New Year's and slipped a check into my hand as I got on the train. A big check. I'll keep in touch he said, meaning money. I felt my eyes go foggy. Poor old bastard: he was wearing my scarf. It was a long grim trip home. Home. So to speak.

Danny. Ivan. The pavements knocking my feet into my knees.

Every month a check from my uncle. A reserved letter explaining I'll get it all when he dies anyway so why not now? I hold nothing against him for all the years he might have helped me: how was he to know until he saw me in his house at Christmas ravaged into tears in front of his silver boxes. I have nothing against him either for hiring a perverted gardener, for how should a man like my uncle be able to spot perversion when he sees it. This takes some learning. I had a quick shabby abortion without shedding a tear, during which I imagined a small, very small fetus in a sailor suit was being whisked out of me: a little fetus eating an apple, pink-cheeked Jimmie. No tears; I simply felt gutted.

Now I go to night school and plow through Shakespeare; I discovered Sir Thomas Browne all by myself; and I turned my hand to the pen ungracefully. During the day I write copy for an advertising agency; my publisher's clothes stand me in good stead, still. And sometimes I pass Danny on the street. We give each other contrived nods of the head—I am all fresh-faced, slept well, fattening up again, with regular hours for sleep and work and study: Danny is crazy-eyed, stooped, white at the mouth, jaunty as ever, flashing gold cuff links and a gleaming stick pin, his pointed shoes passing my sensible ones on the street where we lived. He hands me an abrupt nod of the head in vague greeting. Danny still looks fourteen, with accoutrements. I know I look civilized to him, as I would to Ivan, or subdued to my publisher; just as they would look mad to me, the light gone from their faces. I read a book about shearwaters, how one released in Boston found his way home over the Atlantic. I could not find my way to my mother's door without a map, but in my brain I have homing instincts: why one reaches the edge and doesn't go over, why daylight becomes the natural habitat, why one walks in the sun.

Ivan on your windy street corner at night, your nerves torn, too chic to wrap a scarf around your throat; oh Danny who wants to nuzzle but goes out a predator on the streets; oh little Jimmie so soon to learn the joy of a kiss. Blinking your eyes in the strong light of day. I wonder where you are while I circumnavigate the cliffs on street corners and learn to walk in the sun. Maybe the yearbook was right and I am a born homemaker.

An Insubstantial Father

Tess was on her way to the funeral. A father is a man like any other. But he had curiously come to life when he died, and other men, she supposed, died when they died. The rain flew on the windshield; her brother drove carefully, lost in the mechanics of it. No need to be careful: car accidents are not so purposefully ironic as to kill the son on his way to the funeral of the father done in by a car. Perhaps Max drove carefully to avoid speaking to her. For now that the details in Florida were finished with, they were strangers again. They had been close, going through their father's desk and coming on old photographs of themselves as children which the man in his indifference still had kept in his top drawer. They had ruthlessly thrown everything away including the pictures, but in the late afternoon Max poured her some Scotch in a bathroom tumbler, and kissed her on the cheek; the first kiss since childhood. Pointless to insist on that kiss. She knew he disapproved of, and chose to ignore, her drifting life; he was a conservative married young man, and yet she felt they were alike, both serious and loose-limbed; alike, but as they drove along to the funeral they continued to be unknown to each other. Only, as they passed small inlets of sea on the

46

Connecticut coast, she saw the water darkened with wind: water. She understood nothing of what went on under its surface, but her father had been an oceanographer; not till that minute did she connect his work with her own liking for water. In these ways was he coming alive.

"Will Aunt Louise be there?" Tess asked.

"I suppose so."

"But they hadn't seen each other in years."

"Still." *Wouldn't you come to my funeral?* Yes I guess I would, though sometimes blood is tenuous; you wonder that there is such a thing. Is there really a woman named Louise who says: That was my brother. Wouldn't any man one reads about in the obituary columns do? When I am middle-aged and someone calls up and says: Your brother . . . today . . . accident . . . will I know there is blood between us? It seemed cut off at the source, as though she had drawn her brother from a hat. But this was not so, apparently.

"I still think Mummy should have come," Tess said.

"Daniel wouldn't have wanted her to. An ex-husband is an old shoe."

An ex-father is an old shoe too. No need to cry, ever. Crying in Florida was a last resort, relief. An insubstantial father, bodiless, not a flesh-and-blood father like Daniel who comes home every night and drinks double Scotches. What did her own father drink? He was invisible, always had been, vanished undersea somewhere, occasionally sending up words from the deep to be printed in an oceanographic magazine. Bloodless, boneless, until she had seen the coffin in the Florida funeral parlor: black with a purple shroud, how small a man he must have been to take up so little space in a box. So that time too he had come alive, a small man, bones to lie in a box: that much room he occupied in his skin.

Max turned off the highway in a bleak town that had once housed her father's family. The cemetery was scattered under trees, wet headstones and the serene disorder of country graveyards.

"What if the coffin didn't come on the plane yet?" she asked, wanting to laugh.

"Of course it came."

They could bury an empty box if it didn't, she thought. Once she had found herself on the Washington train to Philadelphia with the body of Douglas MacArthur. But in the Philadelphia station people stood solemnly looking at the wrong track, working up all that emotion for a train that did not carry the casket. But why correct them? The feelings turned toward the wrong train were appropriate. There was nothing more in an empty box than in the box with her father's body inside. In either case she felt nothing. He couldn't be dead who was just coming to shape in her head.

Or if he was dead, what matter? He had been gone since she was four. He had wandered off from them all, was under water and penning the solemnities of the deep. He wrote cursory Christmas letters postmarked from various seaports to remind them that he lived and breathed and saw the light of day. La Jolla, Honolulu, from the Tristan da Cunha Islands, and the Galápagos. She and Max met him once on a street corner in New York, they had planned to meet, but her father stood like a stranger inside the turned-up collar of his trench coat; a man funneled into separation; blank eyes and a heavy, no-longer handsome face. He took Max and Tess on the subway to go to a restaurant, but the wrong subway and they ended up in Queens. The embarrassment of a man who couldn't find his way around. When they finally reached the restaurant, it was a smoky bar where sailors drank, with a room in back, and Italian food. Their father felt at home there, with himself if not with his children; he spread out his arms on the table. There were pictures on the walls of famous people, signed and addressed to the manager, actresses halted in the act of cutting up their veal, fixed on the wall as though the meal were never finished. Their permanence made Tess feel queer; she and Max and her father ate, the plates were cleared, the episode in all its awkwardness was over. But the awkwardness became fastened on her brain, a silence unbroken in trapped mouths.

Max and Tess got out of the car by a small building next to the cemetery, and went indoors where a stout officious man took them aside. Max signed something. Tess went into the ladies' room, which smelled of soap, and brushed her hair, tied the dark scarf back over her ears: too stylish to be appropriate? She untied it and knotted it under her chin as girls in high school did; or as she had done. Unbecoming but to the point; cover your head in the house of the Lord or, if not there—for there were no churches connected with this—then under that portion of the sky belonging to the Lord. His parcel of graveyard. In the waiting room her Aunt Louise had arrived and was filling up silence with her mirthful astonished voice: forced. As though any minute she would say, Max how you've grown, though he gave up growing a good ten years ago. Max stood over her with the deferential bend of his reserved tall head; several times he touched his hair as though to make sure it was neat, though it was too short to be otherwise. Tess went up and shook her aunt's hand; it was not the hand of any woman, but of her father's sister who, like her father, had dropped out of her life swiftly. Then the man behind the desk took them out into the rain where a hearse was parked. Suddenly a Chinese man appeared, hesitantly, under a brown hat. He shook her brother's hand though she knew Max had never set eyes on him before, and when they got into the car to follow the hearse he started on foot up the hill.

"Why don't you ride with us?" Tess asked through the window. The air was muggy and thick. The man got in the back seat with Aunt Louise who said gaily:

"Oh you were a friend of Walter's?"

"Yes yes I was. In Venezuela." Venezuela? "Now I am at Woods Hole. I am a seaman," he added with a dip of his tidy head under the wet hat. "I work for him. A good man, he told me many things."

"*Did* he?" Aunt Louise asked.

The hearse stopped over the edge of the hill and they all got out under trees shedding water like glass. They ducked their heads as though for safety. Six men Tess had never seen in her life slid the coffin out of the hearse and shouldered it. The Chinese man brought up the rear, stooped, as though one of the poles rested on his shoulder. Tess and Max and Aunt Louise followed to the brink of the grave: neat, well dug, wet at the bottom. All the other headstones seemed to look on, streaked under the rain. Perhaps this was the right box after all; it seemed heavy. They suspended it with ropes casually over the drop, and a man in a white collar opened a book in the rain and read. Tess did not listen . . . The Lord giveth and taketh away . . . dust . . . Dust nothing, it was heavy bones in a box. He should have been buried at sea, she thought, nervously, for it was too late. Could she stop it now? In a shroud, into the fathomless water which he had fathomed, sliding, eaten by fish: she thought of Billy Budd: and the oozy weeds about me twist . . .

Too late. Cleverly the ropes lowered the coffin till it obliterated the muddy bottom of the hole. This was a grave. Ashes to ashes. They should have cremated him; this family plot was not his home. Too late however. Someone was throwing down earth with a shovel and it fell with soft splats on the coffin cover. But that's my father, you can't throw dirt like kids filling up a hole.

"Wait!" she called. And then she cried. The Chinese man turned to her and she saw he was old, lined, like an old apple; like a peach because he was yellow. The stones looked on obscurely; everyone was looking at her. And she heard her words in the still air long after they had come from her mouth: Wait!

Aunt Louise asked them to come to her house for lunch, so they agreed to follow her. Max with a restrained flicker of affection in his eyes shook hands with the Chinese man who then walked away under the trees. He looked like a young man from the back, with his hat in his hand and his dark head bare to the sky. Tess and Max drove after their aunt to her white New England house; they were introduced to a man they called Uncle Jim though they had never met him in their lives. There were a lot of children who pell-melled through the house with healthy voices. No room for grief here, shut it up in the mind, though Tess felt her brain form lesions: could she really pick up that shiny glass, ruby with sherry, would the glassy rim of it touch her lips? The rooms smelled too much of roasting lamb to allow for words of grief. Anyway the children had not known their uncle, they stormed around hungry and showing off in front of two grown-up cousins who hadn't much to say for themselves. The sherry sizzled on Tess's tongue, jarring her blood. *So I'm really a walking human being with a hooked-up nervous system. And these are my relatives, we are a family again now that the link that made us so is dead.* How warm it is against the raining day outside, smell of roast and potatoes and fresh biscuits, buttery vegetables. Max and Tess played ping-pong in the basement with the two oldest children: their cousins: Jane and Davie. They ate lunch with their uncle who was perfectly willing to take on these vagabond relations of his wife. When it was time to leave, Tess faltered in the hall putting on her damp coat; for supper this family would eat cold lamb and maybe some soup, the clapboard walls of the house would encase them against the rain and the dark. *Good for them.* She didn't want to stay. She wanted them to go somewhere else, something to intrude. They all said good-bye with promises. Nobody to keep them.

Max drove her back to New York City, where he turned in the rented car and took a plane home to his family in California.

The next day came, mercifully. The night like a cleaver had broken her off from the day before. She saw the light go flat against buildings; bricks locked together under it, windows glinted so that she could no longer see the color of curtains behind them. But chimney pots took the winter sun well: curved in it. Blue jays landed on the fire escape and rotated their heads under boneless feathers; they made her feel how sharp humans are; she was conscious of the machinery in her own neck as she turned her face this way and that, looking. Then she took out the negatives she had saved from the house in Florida and studied them against the light. Reversed like that, outlined, the black skin blameless, eyes shining, the people were unrecognizable to her. She took them to a drugstore to be developed and was told to pick them up in several days. She waited, in suspension.

For the prints revealed what was hidden in the dark expressionless negatives. Here was her father in a tie and jacket, his hand on the back of the chair beside her as a girl of ten, his hand just not touching her arm, and his eyes turned slightly away both from the camera (or photographer, his ex-wife, six years divorced) and from the child. But his mouth: shy and proud, embarrassed really; and the girl—herself—in a white summer dress, puffed sleeves, white socks, and Mary Janes with the tidy strap over the foot, her eyes staring toward her mother who held the camera, her mother whom she knew. She did not look at the awkward man beside her in his too-hot tweed jacket, the sun full on his face, on the tightening lines lifting upward on his forehead. A stranger to her father.

Another photograph: her brother aged twelve surveying his first shotgun and taking (for posterity's sake) mock instructions from his father. Max's eyes fastened on the hands of his father, a square-knuckled hand, strong fingers deftly at work among the intricacies of lock, barrel, trigger. The man was truly engrossed and not at all posing for the camera, his mind as absent from the lens and his ex-wife's face behind the lens as it was from his son's self-conscious gaze. A father to be worshipped, if they had been worshipping children, a man at home with the gun balanced over the crook of his elbow, his shirt open, the blond hairs on his arm standing up golden (if this had been a color photograph) in the chill wind. Behind father and son a rail fence sagged toward the sea;

the photographer, the conscientious mother, had omitted to frame this touching picture with the proper amount of pasture grass, glimpse of sea, spread of sky; there was too much of the father's and son's shirt tails and pants, as far down as the father's hip boots (they were actually going fishing, not hunting—in spite of the gun which was a prop). Still, familiar as Tess was with that landscape, she filled in the background with her own mind, saw, even if it was not in the picture, the ledges in the pasture breaking up through grass and swamping juniper bushes, saw the shore toppling steep and white, the sky swallow-tailing above them. And she saw, in fact, her brother's eyes fixed on the movements of his father's hands; Max had not known this particular aspect of his father's genius—and how could he, as in the last few years they had met only in the city, shaken hands stiffly on the corners of streets where they had arranged to meet. There was more surprise in Max's expression than pride. And the father: he was not in the habit of showing things to his son; he was less aware of any information he was passing on than he was of that pleasure to hold a gun again, under that sky. Yes without a doubt that man belonged in that particular landscape which his ex-wife had neglected to include in the photograph. And he had gone off to the Pacific, Venezuela so they say, Florida . . . There were more photographs telling the same story: embarrassment, surprise, lack of contact (for not in any of them was anyone touching anyone else). What was it? she puzzled. What had made her and Max so peculiarly unequipped for life, with eyes set back far under blond brows. They pushed the world away—scared, defensive eyes, lacking in tenderness, directness, or gaiety. Neither, she realized, was there any photograph of anyone laughing.

So there had been visits, more than she remembered. She was habituated to her mother's saying that their father had ignored them, although she had sent him these pictures which Tess had never seen. I was a girl in a white dress, pretty enough to bring pride into my father's face, and he, coming north, wore too heavy a jacket, forgetting when spring comes to New England. I have eyes identical to Max's, eyes poked back in the head. My life is fixed for good in a photograph and yet I was never allowed to see what it was.

No picture of her father and mother together. Destroyed. Nowhere such a picture; her mother had destroyed them. Blood. Her parents had no blood between them but they gave us blood; yet you would have thought all these years that it was only my mother's. Genes. Dominant and recessive. The bitch.

She had avoided her mother and stepfather for four days after the funeral but one morning the phone jolted her up from sleeping. It was her mother asking her to come to dinner. She said Yes from the recesses of a mind accustomed to pleasing her mother. But when she was awake, she was appalled at the idea of a mother. If her father were alive by death then her mother as a mother was eclipsed. The intimacy of being the child of that woman when she wanted to be the child of that man. Nonetheless she went to dinner: to the tall dim apartment sheltering pianos and stuffed chairs; the dark shine of mahogany furniture, the legs of tables standing slim on the polished floor, the polite arch in the backs of dining-room chairs; gold frames dull in the light; wattled mirrors reflecting the lamps and passing faces: her stepfather, a good lawyer, with weighty things on his mind and showing in his face, her mother with her long hair piled up on her head, her pretty, self-absorbed face. They were gentle with her, which annoyed her, gentle without speaking, speaking of other things.

Daniel mixed double Scotches with soda expertly, pushing up his cuffs gripped in their cuff links before cracking out the ice.

"We hardly saw Max," her mother said.

"He was hardly here. He missed a lot of work, going to Florida. He had to get back. We did go to Florida, you know."

"And his family," said Daniel, who felt a successful stepfather with one stepchild married off. He was always interested in Max's family.

"Well *they* can get along without him for a *little* while. I did think he was looking well, though, didn't you, Tess?"

"Yes he was, considering. Do we have to pretend he came on a pleasure trip?"

"*You*'re looking tired though. We'll send you home early."

"I'm not tired."

"Shall we take our drinks to the table," her mother said. Sitting together they dealt with their utensils. Tess who had always been so at ease with Daniel and her mother. They passed plates stiffly as though in practice for a course in good manners. "Won't you have . . . ?" "Please let me give you . . ." They seemed to have pins in their shoulder bones.

"Tess darling, you must eat more. You really have gotten too thin."

"I'm eating."

"Where will you go on your vacation?" Daniel asked.

"I'm thinking of going out to see Max next month," she said, thinking of it for the first time.

"Oh how sweet of the boy to invite you! You really

must go. You'll love the baby. You haven't seen her, have you?"

"You know I haven't, Mummy."

"Yes, I forgot you haven't visited them since they moved. Do go. It would be so good for you."

"It's not for my health. I'd like to see Max under more normal conditions."

"Tess, I think you're being a little flippant with your mother."

"Yes I am. He was my father, you know."

"He was my husband once too," her mother said suddenly.

Daniel got up with abrupt tactfulness. "I'll leave you two to talk."

Tess felt sick with the intimacy in the room, two women, mother and daughter, flesh and blood, ordered to talk about a man in their lives.

"Darling, I know it must have been hard on you."

"It wasn't hard. What's hard is now." Some old crowbar of closeness to her mother pried her open. "I wish he were alive!" she said, in tears over her plate.

"And so do I."

"You! You forgot him as soon as he left. You made us hate him, you sent him all the pictures of us. We never had any to remind us."

"Listen, whenever you saw your father it was because I made him come see you. I wrote and begged him to come, made arrangements for you to meet him."

"He didn't forget us. He had pictures of us in his desk."

"Having pictures is one thing, paying attention to you is another."

"He didn't belong down there. He belonged in New England. We drove him out."

"He went of his own free will."

But Tess sat. As though with an ax the years broke around her and she saw him on a street corner in the rain looking after them: they in a car. When was that? She and Max looking out the back window. He was waving. They were leaving him, leaving him for good, she could see that by his face. But after that he ignored them. Or felt alone. Came to visit out of love, or at her mother's request. Whichever.

She looked up and saw her mother crying.

"Do you just forget, Mummy?"

"No, you don't. I wish he were alive too."

Tess reached out and touched her mother's arm. Something she had never done before. Her mother turned over her hand and took Tess's fingers in her grip.

Daniel came in and patted them both on the backs. They smiled all around and went back to the living room where Daniel built a fire. They sat refuged by its warmth. Then Tess saw her mother's feet; the ankles were swollen. Still she was a beautiful woman. She survived age. And suddenly Tess wanted her mother to be old so that she could pity her her age, love her for the lines and swellings.

When Tess got up to leave, Daniel gave her money for a taxi; the fire simmered in the grate. There were no hardships in this house, there was comfort. But it was bleak; shadowy rooms dim and too large to fill, empty corners in the shadows where the lamps did not reach. She saw her mother, small, and aging before her eyes because she had seen those ankles, putting her hand to her hair, standing in the large room not wanting to let her daughter go. As the elevator hissed down in its shaft Tess stood elated: age lay on them all, brutal, swift, only noticed when it was gripped by the mind. Oblique: one could not see it straight on.

That night she phoned Max in California. "Max!" she called, her voice threading out across America. They had stood in the Miami airport heading north for the funeral, their father's house disposed of, belongings destroyed. It had been hot; clouds thickened, forerunners of disasters, storms, tornadoes. The air like a hand over her mouth. Heavy sun on Max's forehead, sweat drawn out from the skin. A color of skin goldeningly shone in the light, pale hairs at his temples; very much alive. Someone had seen her father just so (the old Chinese man, she now knew). By no power of the mind had she been able to imagine Max's face gone from this sun. "Max!" she called. "This is Tess."

"Hello, Tess. What's up?"

"You know, I have vacation next month. I'd love to come see you."

"Sure thing. We'd like that." A paradigm of understatement, her brother. "You haven't seen Lisa." Her niece. Cells. Heredity. Her brother's fair hair; she had seen photographs of Lisa.

"I'll let you know when I can come."

"We don't need much warning, just enough to meet you."

Conversation. How is everyone, give them my love. She heard her voice winging off; but his winged back.

Night over New York. Her friends, her job, everything had been like chips of colored glass; though she had refused to believe she could be upset by the death of a man she hardly knew. The cessation of an absence. Still her life was broken, but colored, reminding her of its intact brightness from weeks before the accident. She sat and looked at her hand under the lamp: at the back of it: for lines. A young hand. A girl.

Breakthrough

The hospital doors were kept unlocked. Nevertheless the effect on Alex White was the same as though they were locked. Every day he told himself that he could sign out to escape this fear of imprisonment, and every day he knew they would not let him go as they considered him harmful to himself. He did not think he was harmful to himself. Least of all to himself. He was harmful to women, to his parents, to strangers. In fact a menace to them all. But never to himself.

But he had unfortunately said to a nurse that he wished he were not alive. There was a distinction, in his mind, between wishing one were not alive—that is, wishing he had not been born—and wishing to kill oneself. But the distinction, especially as he made it several days later and very defensively, to his doctor, was not at all clear to the authorities. And so Alex was not able to sign himself out of a voluntary hospital for Mental Health. And as long as he was in the hospital, it cheered him up that it was called for Mental Health and not for Mental Illness. A small degree of his optimism was based on this objective observation.

The windows of the hospital looked out over an unfamiliar neighborhood in New York: small buildings, a church tower, a busy avenue with a subway stop on the corner. Every morning he looked out of the lounge window to see all the people on their way to work charging down the subway steps as he had charged down similar steps on the Lower East Side. Fortunate people! Harassed, exhausted, overheated under the unremitting fans of the subway, fans redistributing the same hot air, but free people, strong people, perhaps even able to concentrate on the *Times*. While he, Alex White, a city patient, jobless, broken, was not able to follow through with a conversation, pay attention to a news report on the television, and knew for a fact that an unearthly fear had kept him out of subways for three weeks before he entered the hospital. Yes with wonder and a kind of compassion he watched those people every morning drop into the subway entrance. It was like a gate to heaven.

On the opposite corner he saw a newsstand and there people bought with no effort their papers and magazines and even had brief conversations with each other as they struggled to reach down a copy of *Encounter* or *Playboy*. Yes, they spoke with strangers in the sun on a busy corner while he, Alex White, had not spoken to a friend in a month and could not bring himself to make a friend in the hospital for fear of their knowledgeable eyes. Yes, decidedly these other patients knew more than was called for, knew the bottom and the unwary hazard of minds and bodies shot to hell. He could not dissemble before these patients, and he had not been able, since he had ceased to be qualified for the subways, to dissemble before anyone out there, before strangers at a newsstand even. Awful, absurd! But he had done it, he had babbled to the strangers reaching for their papers, challenged them, and gone away without being able to buy a paper of his own. From the window he watched them all now with tenderness for them. They were protected from him, all over New York they bought and read and pushed and rode subways while he had dropped out of their lives abruptly. They were flesh and blood, they felt dimes in their palms and sweat around the forehead; he was insubstantial now, all brain and nerves, like a wire figure of the nervous system.

Nonetheless he made friends in the hospital, inadvertently, in open moments when the wire figure filled out and he felt himself to be made, momentarily, of flesh. Nino, his Italian roommate, dawned on him perhaps twice a day, with a face more Oriental than European, soft slanted eyes and an immobile harmless face. Mostly Nino spoke about his wife and how she would come back to him, or he advised Alex to get married and to marry a woman who loved the home and had no ambitions. It sounded like a good idea to Alex, but as his present girl friend was an assistant editor on a magazine and as he had thought, at odd moments, of marrying her, he argued with Nino. This daily grappling with the idea of women's rights refreshed Alex—or more likely, Nino's point of view refreshed him, for he would like to have adapted it to his own and so be furnished with an excuse for ridding himself of the haughty cool eyes of Charlotte which focused on him from his own difficult brain. For though he did not believe he loved her, she appeared hourly in the mind, and four times a week in person, as the only possible hope. Both in his thinking and during visiting hours she brought back his total self, reminded him of the days when he sweated and laughed and took his shoes to the shoemaker. Perhaps the thought of Nino's wife did the same for Nino. But the exchanges between the two men were brief, for Alex's mind wandered into thoughts of Alex and cut Nino out altogether. Their arguments fleshed them both into life, but temporarily.

He flirted with Michele. That was natural, for most of the patients were older: men who lay in their beds all day, men who prowled the halls, a few women on canes, women who wept without relief in the lounge chairs, and a small group of Jewish women who knitted and crocheted and worked on crossword puzzles by the hour; and many of them disdainful of Alex's shabby clothes and Michele's sloppiness. But he and Michele kept up an unrelenting flirtation without the slightest real attraction for each other. Michele, with bad eyesight and lank pale hair, disheveled, sleepy with medication, self-effacing, self-pitying, pretty, and begging for his sympathy, she received none of it, only his attention, his concentrated effort to remember he was a man and not a wire figure. What she wanted or got from him did not concern him. Every day, in his jeans and jersey, he walked into the lounge where one person at least—Michele, with her jerky uncertain eyes—saw him consistently as a man on legs. She was, she told him in confidence, a virgin.

The staff, the nurses and aides, who passed in and out of his days, changing every eight hours and turning his case, every shift, over to new nurses and aides, did not count as his friends. They were magically solid. He spoke to them out of a great distance, from himself and from the other patients, in hours when Nino's arguments and Michele's watchfulness did nothing for him. The staff were Godlike in their ability to remain above water while he felt sinking; they did not go under with him. But he did not trust them with his thoughts, having been, as he saw it, betrayed in his confidence about wishing he were not alive. Sometimes Mr. Berne, an aide—who came to work in a crash helmet—or Mrs. Alberti, a nurse, played cards with him, or Scrabble, or ping-pong; they came the closest to being his friends. But the nurse he preferred was Miss Bergholz, and she was indifferent to him, and spoke with a cool precision which made him awkward. His trouble with women, he knew, may have been that he chose the Miss Bergholzes, and then shied back from them; but of all the staff, still he preferred her.

On yellow paper pinned above his bed in his own disjointed handwriting were these lines from Herman Melville: "For in tremendous extremities human souls are like drowning men; well enough they know they are in peril; well enough they know the causes of that peril;—nevertheless, the sea is the sea, and these drowning men do drown."

Alex had been in the hospital one week to the day and was feeling the absorption of that life, its drifting quality, as though he were on a long sea voyage. He was standing out of the sun on the roof. The Beatles screamed from a phonograph with a split needle; someone was using the punching bag in the gym, where the door was propped open so that the sound, confident and regular, came to him in the muggy shade. From here he could see the church tower, a pink crazy fretted tower with a round clock face as adorable as a child. Michele, with a badminton racket in her hand, unsteadily stooped to take off one sandal and then the other, racking her brains for something to say; that he could see, for suddenly, like a boy at camp, he never wanted to leave this heat, this racket of music, this soothing *whamp* of the punching bag, and rose euphorically even above Michele, soared, feeling himself like a great red sun rising over a pile of garbage. Michele persisted, and happily, from that height, he acquiesced.

"Come on, Alex, let's play."

She ran out ahead of him, into the sun, waving her racket at the net. An old black woman sitting in a chair lifted her eyes casually, looking at Michele, as Alex was looking at Michele, and seeing a slight, young girl in her bare feet prancing delicately on the hot tiles. Larry, whom Alex called Prince Myshkin, an adolescent with a scrawny body and a holy though pimply face, was pointing out an airplane; he waved and smiled softly at it, then shouldered an imaginary rifle and took aim, carefully, in the sun. Alex, a racket in his hand, stepped onto the court, feeling the new intense heat after the shade, and a dim awful certainty that this serenity was manic, wrong, was the passage into a fall, that he was stepping into the fall already, that Michele and Michele's eyes were pulling him down again into a struggle to be merely human. The absurd little church clock said two forty-five or thereabouts; the sun was blanketing hot and still, as though fixed on that particular roof; and Larry, having shot down his plane, stood with his holy face just out of range of Michele's racket. She dropped the birdie, she swung and sent it flying; Mrs. Alberti was emerging from the shade with a new patient at her side. Alex swung, the sweat had sprung out on his forehead, the new patient was a dark-haired cowlike girl of perhaps sixteen, she was gazing down and walking with a swaying motion, dragging her feet; for Mrs. Alberti's sake he swung carefully with straightened wrist, as in tennis, at the white birdie in front of his face. He missed. The new patient laughed, a round warm secret laugh. She had been watching all the time, from under very thick and very dark lashes. Alex threw down his racket and cursed.

"Oh come on, Alex!" Michele was still leaping on the hot tiles, flinging up the soot-blackened bottoms of her feet at which Larry was staring attentively. There was irritation in her voice: don't spoil my fun. Alex, to spoil it, turned to the new patient. She stood, with drooping shoulders and slack arms, close to Mrs. Alberti, so close that as Alex approached she took Mrs. Alberti's hand.

"Who he?" she asked with her eyes just off Alex's face.

(Oh my God, an idiot. But she had blue, pretty, shadowed eyes.)

"Alex, this is Julia."

"Hello Julia. Would you like to play badminton?"

"No." And she turned to Mrs. Alberti who, disengaging her hand, was about to leave them. "Where you go?"

"I'm going back downstairs, Julia."

"You come back?"

"I'll be back at three thirty to bring you downstairs."

"He come too?"

"Yes, everyone from the fifth floor comes down."

"When?"

"At three thirty."

"Me too?"

"You too, Julia."

"You be back?"

"Yes. I told you I'd be back. When did I say I'd be back?"

With a swift, secret smile and averted eyes, Julia said: "I don't know."

"When did I say, Julia?"

"At three thirty." And her smile included Alex and the sun and Michele and everything under the sun, a steady smile under the slow purposeful move of her eyes so that Alex felt like putting his hands under the weight of dark hair and pulling her into a hug. She asked all the right questions. He asked them himself, to himself, when he was afraid. This lovely, heavy, cowlike girl with her serene and beautiful smile was afraid.

Alex and Julia stood together in the shade. He lit a cigarette. He was no longer euphoric, no longer rising, but neither was he falling. He stood calmly, sweating, with his back to the court. In the gym he could see, over Julia's slumped shoulder, Michele dancing limberly, still in her bare feet, to an old Beatles song which brought up for him other hot summers and deadly deadly girls squirming in front of him in crowded places. Julia gazed past him with her shy, now less open, but effortless smile; a black handbag hung on her shoulder.

"This a hospital?"

"Yes, this is a hospital."

"I be here forever?"

"No," he said, and felt his brain give a jerk. Yesterday a patient had been sent off to a state hospital; he himself saw no possibility of release into the outside world; state hospital stood in front of his mind always, like the black end of a long tunnel when one expected sunlight, a place where he would be shut away for good. "No, you won't be here forever."

"You be here forever?"

"No, I won't be here forever. No one's here forever."

"Why?"

Why? If not here, then the state hospital where you get shipped in an ambulance without even a chance to step on real city pavements before you go in. Why? But this was a short-term hospital, you couldn't stay more than three months. "You can't stay here forever. That's the law."

"I be here forever?"

"No, Julia, you can't." Give her the same hope you give yourself. "That's the law."

"That's the law," she repeated. "You my friend?"

"I'd like to be your friend, Julia. Do you know my name?"

"No."

"Alex."

"Alex. Take my hand."

He hesitated. Michele often, when playing cards, rested a free hand near him on the card table; once she said, when he brushed her fingers with his arm, "Hey, no physical contact between patients." That too was the law. Alex put out his hand and took Julia's strongly, because he knew this was not absolutely right. She spoke oddly, she was a child in her mind, she walked without any picture of her own young woman's body, she was like a tall slightly fat four-year-old; but she had pale-blue secret gazing eyes and that steady smile like a woman constantly in love; he took her hand as though she were a child; but she was beautiful.

Michele came up at an angle to them.

"Hello there. Ready to go down? I feel great, dancing *does* something to me."

"Michele, this is Julia. She's new on the floor." He held onto Julia's hand. But quietly, as though not to disturb his, she undid her own and reached for Michele's.

"You my friend?"

"Sure I'm your friend. We're all friends here."

Face it, man, Alex was saying to himself, she takes everybody's hand. She's simple-minded, retarded. She has no more use for your hand; they're all the same, yours, Mrs. Alberti's, Michele's. And the three of them left the badminton court, passed the phonograph which was scratching out the Supremes, and rode off with Mrs. Alberti in the elevator away from their visit to the sun. Alex was thinking of ways to escape.

That night Charlotte visited, as she did every visiting hour. His parents, who lived in San Francisco, threatened to visit but never did. Tonight Charlotte, bearing her leather satchel full of important work, sat beside him, coifed, pretty, with strong eye make-up and her stern little jaw lifted toward him.

"You seem happy today," she said, putting a cigarette into a holder and bringing all her intelligence into her voice as though she had noticed something about him he had not seen in himself.

"I'm very happy. I played badminton on the roof."

"That sounds nice. Not so afraid anymore?"

"Afraid of what?"

"Oh you know, last time you were afraid you'd never get out, or of state hospitals, something like that."

(I be here forever?) "There's always that possibility, Charlotte."

"Have you asked your doctor when you'll get out?" (Every time the same question, and he'd been in only a week.) "You should start asking him."

(What is there to get out for? You? For you, Charlotte?) Alex saw Nino across the lounge, Nino's priest-brother with his arm around Nino, the two pale faces bent together, talking, talking, perhaps about Nino's wife. Would she come back to him? She had, Nino told Alex yesterday, wanted him to make more money; that was ambition, that was no good in Nino's terminology; he quit the merchant marine to stay home with her, but he could not make a go of it as a salesman; she insisted on more money. "Women should love the home and that's all," Nino had persisted with stubborn certainty. Nonetheless he wanted her back. Alex watched him and the priest; more wisdom there than in an assistant editor, than in Charlotte with her satchel; he could not bring himself to

69

call it, correctly, an attaché case. These arguments with Nino picked up speed after visiting hours when Nino had seen Charlotte with her leather satchel. "Stay away from ambitious women, sonny." But Alex knew he would go back to Charlotte; there she was, with her literary gossip, her own money. She would wait for him. He would go to her. And he remembered standing out of the sun on the roof, feeling himself rising, then falling, Michele's demands, Charlotte's, garbage garbage, play badminton with me, hit the little white birdie, ask your doctor when you'll get out, come back to me, make love to me, touch my hand on the card table, be sane for me, be a man for me, see me dancing on my bare feet, see me with my case full of important work, look at me, love me. Also across the room Julia sat, alone; her parents were not allowed to visit her yet. She looked at the floor indifferently, with her head lowered. She wore a string of pearls, her hair was tied back in a bun like a woman, she wore a soft green dress; she was grown-up in spite of herself. In her lap lay her black purse; she gripped the strap. Charlotte was talking.

"You'll never get out if you're so casual about it, Alex. I've never seen you so passive."

"Oh shut up, Charle. You haven't any idea why I'm in here; why worry about my getting out." His voice lifted, Nino looked his way. Mr. Berne, on the prowl, passed by studiously, cracking the joints in his fingers; he gave Alex one of his mirthless but tender smiles; on the chart tonight he would write that Alex White did not have a pleasant visit. Julia smiled suddenly at the raising of Alex's voice, got up, and approached them with her rolling, foot-dragging walk. She stood in front of Charlotte.

"You pretty."

"Why thank you."

Alex introduced them, but Julia turned away and followed Mr. Berne. In the doorway she said something to him, and he took her hand. Alex shrugged.

"Visiting hours are over," announced a nurse's voice. Alex took Charlotte to the elevators. She had put on her most understanding face and he kissed her without joy. He was back into his nerves, a wire figure.

There was no joy but he would have liked very much to have been able to leave with Charlotte and perhaps find a better life among the collapses of the old. Leaning against the wall in the corridor he heard a dime drop in the pay phone and Julia's voice. "Daddy? You come tomorrow? . . . I go home, when? . . . Who home? Mommy home? . . ." He listened with attention. There was distress in her voice, it raised without breaking, like a lament. "When I be home? . . . You take me home." Alex took out a nickel and went over to the booth; she was likely to get caught in the middle. But abruptly she said: "Good-bye, Daddy." There was absolutely no difference between the words she used to her father and the words in her head; speaking meant little to her, the straight exposure of the straight workings of her mind. She gave Alex her sweet and timid smile.

They took walks up and down the hall, Julia and Alex.

"I a trouble at home. I nervous, in my heart."

"You'll get better, Julia."

"My parents come tonight?"

"I don't know, Julia. You should ask your doctor."

"You go home soon?"

"Someday I'll go home. You'll go home too."

"I no go home. I be here forever."

"You won't be here forever."

"Why?"

"No one stays forever."

"Why?"

"It's the law. No one stays here more than three months."

"I no stay forever?"

"No."

"Why?"

"You know why. What did I tell you?"

And with a sideways smile she said: "It's the law."

You be here forever? In his bed he wondered. He lay thinking of Miss Bergholz with her indifferent occasionally soft face—soft when she spoke with Julia—her myopic eyes, her dancelike movements; thought of how Mrs. Alberti approached him to talk, but how he had to approach Miss Bergholz. He had to approach Charlotte, that day in an office when he was peddling his political masterpiece and she, assistant editor, sat—behind a desk cluttered with urgently important papers—casually, under his unsteady eye; "We'll look this over, Mr. White." I'll look you over, Mr. White. "If I have any time later I'll talk with you," said Miss Bergholz with the attentive turn of her balanced head as she passed him in the hall on her way to more pressing matters; she was thirty-five if she was a day. Michele set her hand near his on the card table under Mr. Berne's eye; no physical contact between patients, Mr. White, she laughed. I feel so *great* dancing; her private joy while he stood outside, having missed the birdie she had served him. We'll look this over, Mr. White. If I have any time later. You my friend? You be here forever? Well would he? Miss Bergholz's cold look when he passed her in the hall. A wish to crawl on his knees to Mrs. Alberti. Too late, she went home at four. Though he never talked to her, just played cards, ping-pong, delaying the urgent questions in his brain till evening when Miss Bergholz had no time to listen. You my friend? Miss Bergholz are you my friend? Alex turned over and looked at Nino. Nino slept on his side, tonight painfully, like a man who has just been punched. A sinewy arm was flung sideways from his chest; he snored apprehensively.

Would Alex be here forever? In a state hospital, away from badminton, Michele, Mrs. Alberti, away from the joyless laugh and piercing eyes of Mr. Berne, away from these—yes!—friends? He was distrustful, he knew that, the doctor had told him so, he believed it, a deep internal mistrust, of locked doors and state hospitals, of doctors and women, of subways and strangers, of himself. He was all nerves and no soul; he had a soul like a washline, cluttered, clean, but vulnerable. Not such a bad guy, but he gets dirty in a hurry. If you leave my soul out too long it fades, it gets dirty. I distrust the very sky.

He turned over and breathed heavily. His mind reeled over. Thoughtfully he told himself that Mrs. Alberti and Mr. Berne sought him out, she in the daytime, he at night. He could count on them. The evidence lay with them, not with Miss Bergholz, who snubbed him. Nonetheless it was the snub which convinced him. With resignation he went on mistrusting. You be here forever? Perhaps just that.

They took walks up and down the hall, Julia and Alex.

("You take a great interest in Julia," Miss Bergholz said.)

"I be home my birthday?"

"When's your birthday?"

73

"September three."

"Yes, you'll be home by then."

"How you know?"

"You should ask your doctor, Julia."

"I no go home." She lumbered, stood up against the wall, smiled serenely over his shoulder. "I not frightened anymore."

"What were you frightened about?"

"Dunno. I not frightened now. When I go home?"

("When do you think you'll be getting out Alex?" Charlotte asked.

"Are you so sick of waiting?"

"Oh Alex, you can trust me, can't you? I'm not sick of waiting, but I do think you should speak with the doctor."

"The doctor's no help at all. What have you been doing with yourself?"

"There was a party at Raymond's last night."

His bewilderment. Healthy men in a healthy world.)

Julia no longer carried her black bag over her shoulder. The first night without it, Miss Bergholz said: "So you've decided to stay with us for a while, Julia?" Yes, Julia said. There was a nice quality in Miss Bergholz's voice as she asked that. But Miss Bergholz would not meet Alex's eye in this happy moment. Julia no longer asked if her parents were coming. Julia said to Alex: "You my friend" without the question mark. They walked in the hall. Her feet dragged and she swayed from side to side, her dark hair fallen over her cheeks. Finally she said:

"I happy here. Here my friends."

She liked Mr. Berne especially. "He no make fun of me."

"Do I make fun of you, Julia?"

"Yes," with a soft averted smile. "You tell me I pretty."

"Well you are pretty, very pretty."

"Don't!"

"If you'd just wear your hair up every day, you'd be beautiful."

"Don't. You no say that. I listen to my father. He tell me what to do. I no talk to you. You not my father."

And for the rest of the day she would not speak to Alex except to say: "You not my father." But by evening they paced the hall again.

"Aren't I your friend, Julia?"

"You my friend. But you no tell me what I do. I obey my father."

(If you don't go into business, son, you'll never make anything of yourself. Alex, you *could* have shaved: his mother's voice over lunch in Central Park, their yearly visit. From across three thousand miles he felt their enmity.)

"You not my father."

"No, Julia. I'm your friend."

They had wandered into her room. Julia stood by the sink and saw herself in the mirror. Her head back and slightly sideways, she surveyed herself through half-closed eyes with the confident sensual scrutiny of all beautiful women confronted with themselves in mirrors.

"My father not forget me." She turned around and tears fell out of her eyes. He was surprised to see her cry. "I love my home. I a pain, here." And she pressed her hands against her breasts, which rose under the pale green material of her dress.

"You'll be going home soon, Julia."

"No. I be here forever." She continued to cry, without effort, surprise, or fear.

"You won't be here forever. You know that."

75

"Why?"

"Because . . . Julia, you'll get *better,* you'll feel *better,* you'll get well!"

"No. I a trouble at home. I a pain, here."

But before she could touch her heart again he gripped her elbow. She shivered, and the tears fell out of her eyes like drops from a medicine dropper.

"You'll get better. You won't be here forever."

"It's the law," she said with a glimmer of happiness.

"No no. Never mind the law. It's you, you'll get better. You'll get better, Julia. You'll go home. You'll go home, Julia, and you'll be better." His voice was pitched, manic, edged with frenzy. He heard his words against his head as though they had been thrown there, impersonally, from a loudspeaker. But they cost him an effort; his throat was tight from rasping them out.

Unaccountably the tears had vanished into Julia's skin; only her eyes were shiny, like glass under water. "Yes. I go home soon." Swaying, she stepped into the hall, smiling down the length of it. "Walk. Come on, Alex, walk."

They were both smiling foolishly.

By the elevators, as they took their walk, Alex spotted a sign hung on one of them: Temporarily Out of Service. He put it around his neck and took Julia into the lounge where they sat with Nino.

"What that say?" Julia asked.

"Temporarily out of service, that's me."

She laughed her round sweet laugh. Nino began to laugh also, a scratchy small laugh. "You're a card, Julia. You're wonderful."

And suddenly it occurred to Alex that everyone loved Julia. She brought the other patients cups of coffee, she sat beside the women knitting, she pulled up her chair when Michele and Alex played cards and watched them blissfully; even Michele liked Julia. Miss Bergholz was soft with her; Mr. Berne sat with her in front of the television set, neither one speaking, but their heads close together and her hand on his wrist. She was not only special to him, who wanted to spend every minute with her. She was a special person. All by herself she was special. And yet she had chosen him to walk with in the halls; he was the one who supplied her with the answers. In his words he was right, right for her, perhaps for himself; it was only in his thinking that he was wrong. But his answers to her had not come out of his thinking; they bloomed in his mind, in that part of him that longed to trust. Nino was laughing again with Julia, and the tears rose in Alex's eyes, easily, as though a wind had struck them. So after all there was no total definition of himself as a mistrustful person. Some small portion of him had supplied simple answers to a simple girl, and that portion had sustained him for weeks. It was like locating peace; and that peace was giving him inexplicable turmoil. He wept in front of Nino and Julia.

Late the next afternoon a walk was planned. Alex, a fat woman whose legs met at the knees, Michele, and Julia were accompanied by Mr. Berne. Mr. Berne was in an especially cheerful mood though he had come to work early to take them out, and though he looked tired. "You look tired," Alex said to him. "I only slept an hour, in the park," he told Alex as they passed through the front door onto the street. It was Alex's first time out in the three weeks he had been in the hospital. He was heady and tentative; he kept beside Mr. Berne, loving him for his night in the park and for his **motorcycle**, which he pointed out to Alex, parked at the curb. Someone like himself. Only Mr. Berne was a graduate student, he earned the right to bum occasionally, while he, Alex, bummed all the time. It occurred to Alex to ask Mr. Berne more about himself, but Mr. Berne went ahead with Margaret, the fat woman, leaving Alex between Michele and Julia. It was Michele's first time out also, though Julia, advancing quickly, had already been out; also her parents had been told they could now visit her. Julia spoke of going home soon all day.

"Oh, it all looks crazy," cried Michele. "I'm afraid to cross the street."

"No you're not, Michele. I'll hold onto you."

"No physical contact between patients," she jeered.

No physical contact between patients. We'll look this over, Mr. White. They passed the newsstand which Alex watched every morning from the lounge window. They looked odd, all these people. He took Michele's arm as they crossed the avenue. Julia no longer asked for his hand, or anyone's; she was going home soon. Across the street Alex forgot and kept hold of Michele's arm. "She your friend?" Julia asked. He saw her blue eyes aslant with sunlight. He had not seen her eyes in the sun since the first day on the roof. They were pale and shaded as bottle glass. Here was the subway entrance. Every day Charlotte took the subway to work. I forgive you Charlotte for your attaché case. Call it by its right name. She is a businesswoman. All these people managed so well on the street. He released Michele's arm. It was summer and girls ran in the street, jaywalking; cars with their tops down shot off from the stoplight behind them; the awning over a tobacco store flapped lazily up in the sun and settled like a great striped bird; in the window of an apartment yellow curtains dragged out and fell back over the sill; all the patients and Mr. Berne drew up at the next block, obediently, foolishly, as though lost. Not one of them, except Mr. Berne, could have pulled himself together to jaywalk in the sun. The streets were a carnival at which they had no place. This is the real, or outside world, Alex wondered, looking through dazed eyes. So many weeks in his curtained bed, the cold hallway, the antiseptic lounge. The heat from the sidewalks, the smell of exhaust, women with grocery packages. Charlotte hated to cook. He was afraid.

The light changed and they moved out behind Mr. Berne to cross the street. Alex took Julia's hand. On the other side they fell behind. He put his hand up behind her heavy hair and took her neck gently, stroking her under the dark bun of hair. They were half a block behind the others; he moved his face close to her and with his other palm turned her chin towards him. With a shrug of her shoulders she shied away from him. "Don't," she said in her even, happy voice. "Mr. Berne," she called and moved ahead. Alex watched her slow, foot-heavy walk; the clasp of her beads was over on one side of her neck; it shone in the sun. On the next street corner he caught up with them all. "Julia," he began.

"You not bother me. You a trouble to me. Not bother me!" And she asked for Mr. Berne's hand. Alex walked the rest of the way with Michele, and neither one spoke. He felt unfit and walked with his mouth open, to exhibit his stupidity.

Visiting hours were almost over. Charlotte hung on his arm, forcing from him his admission that he had treated her badly in the spring. "I couldn't help it, Charle, I was falling apart. Can't you forgive a little?" The bright long hallway lengthened and shortened as they walked, past the open and closed doors; he had a glimpse of the fat woman Margaret crying on her bed. Even Margaret was nicer to him than Charlotte. "You used to rape me when I was working at home," she repeated. "Forget what I did then, can't you? I was in rotten shape." Excuses excuses, but why did she use the word rape. Julia's parents, two Italians with worried faces, came out of her room and approached him. "Will you give me a chance to explain," he was saying to Charlotte. But he knew they were about to speak to him.

Julia's parents confronted him outside the men's room door.

"Julia tells us you've been bothering her."

"Me? I didn't mean to bother her. I'm very fond of her." (Charlotte's face lifted.) "What did she say?"

They were utterly straightforward, with deprecating stubbornness.

"She tells us you did some nasty things. She's very young."

Not the trace of an accent. Perhaps second-generation Italians, unlike Nino, who was born in Naples. Marry a woman who'll take care of the home.

"I'd never . . . I'm very sorry if . . ."

"We spoke to the nurse on duty." (Oh my God, Miss Bergholz.) "And she says you shouldn't talk to Julia for a while."

"But I'm very fond . . ."

Julia came out of her room and shot him a sly, lovely glance.

"You tell him, Mommy? He not bother me." And she called her parents back into her room.

Charlotte observed him with her lifted face. "What nasty things have you been up to, Alex?"

"Look, I like the girl very much."

"Apparently. But this *is* a hospital, you keep telling me."

No physical contact between patients. You used to rape me. Julia tells us you've been bothering her. All perfectly true. They had reached, in their walking, the elevators. The Out of Service sign still hung on its string. He could no longer remember what sense of humor had prompted him to hang it on himself; but he remembered Julia's laugh when he told her what it said. To invoke that humor, which was eclipsed now, he took the sign off and strung it on his neck.

"You're a perfect child," Charlotte said; and was gone.

The lights mercilessly exposed every doorway; they cut shadows and were harsh on faces. He went quickly past the nurses' station where Miss Bergholz, on a stool, was writing in a chart. Perhaps that he had bothered Julia. In his own room Nino was sleeping, askew, on the bed. Alex pulled the curtains around his own, though the air was thick with heat. He read Melville's words. These drowning men do drown. I'll sign out of this place even though I am afraid of the streets and the people who know how to jaywalk. I wish I were not alive though I'll never tell anyone again that I feel that. I am a cripple. Julia. Suddenly he wondered if, in Italian, she could speak whole sentences. He was glad he could not speak Italian to find out. He preferred her relentless half-sentences; they were like the essentials of his own mind. They were everything he never dared say. He was drowning.

"I'm not getting up," he was screaming at Nino. Daylight, morning was at the window behind his blue curtains; through the break in them he saw Nino's concerned face, then his back as he set off for breakfast. Alex believed he would never eat again. Mrs. Alberti was sitting on the bed; she urged him to get up, she pulled back the curtains; with a little effort to sit up he would have been able to see the crazy little church tower from the window; but he could not make the effort. Mrs. Alberti had freckles all over her tanned face, and an elegantly thin nose; she couldn't be more than twenty-two. Nonetheless she was the nurse, while he, at twenty-four, was the patient. Was this fear his payment for having loved a girl unlike all other girls? For having intruded on her with his clumsy filthy habits. You used to rape me. He remembered the stubborn eyes of her parents. She was a girl still! Would always be a girl; he hoped she would be home by September third; perhaps being, as he saw her, retarded, she would be sent on to another hospital. Tears ripped out of his eyes. "God I'm rotten," he cried up at Mrs. Alberti's face. He wanted to ask for her hand, as Julia would have asked. But he was not, he knew, as honest as Julia; only the same impulses were there, the abbreviated sentences. Mrs. Alberti was bringing him his medicine; it must be ten o'clock. He fell into a heavy sleep and woke to see his doctor, the big dark head and ominous eyes, the white coat open over a blue shirt. Jesus, help me.

"I've increased your medication. That may be why you're so sleepy."

"I want to get up. I just can't."

"Take it easy for today. By tomorrow you'll be on your feet again."

Help me, doctor. He went off into sleep, sinking from the sight of his doctor's face; he tried to keep his eyes on that face. He slept.

Miss Bergholz was sitting on the edge of the bed. The lights were on.

"Try to get up for dinner, Alex."

"I can't get up."

"You've been asleep all day. Try getting up."

Her face was unusually soft. In a blur he saw her face, her round often haughty now tender face, he saw her two gold earrings with a little chip of amber hanging on each one; the little chip barely swung as she moved her head. He wondered if she felt them on her ears at all. The light came through the amber and set a small patch of yellow against her throat. He felt he knew her; it was all he thought. He got up slowly, dizzily; something like heat flushed up his arms. She took him by one of those arms. He asked her to hold onto him until he was standing. Then like an old old man he made his way along the hallway, braced against the wall, with her hand resting on his elbow as though they were going to church. The medicine was too strong for him, he must protest about it; they had reduced him to an animal and could do anything to him in this state. Miss Bergholz got him seated in the dining room across from Michele. Somewhere in this room was a young girl he must not speak to, though he couldn't remember why not. Something about himself, something rotten and sordid, something to do with her youth and his disgusting rotten habits. He did not look around for her, though in some obscure corner of his brain he knew that it would do him good to see her face. But Miss Bergholz came back and he was led out of the dining room. He had not eaten a thing, and once again he crept along, leaning on the walls, and Miss Bergholz held his arm.

"I must learn to work," he said to her, disturbed by the

83

indistinct memory of having done something wrong. That very young girl Julia—Julia!—had turned him away.

"I think you should learn to relax."

That entered his head like a pin.

"Your doctor wants you to sleep off the medicine and take it easy for a while."

She told him to, and so he would do it.

"Will you be back?"

"I'll look in on you later."

He slept heavily, dreaming of streets.

By the next day he was more accustomed to the medicine and got up in the morning, though wearily, but mellowed. They were not, after all, reducing him to an animal. His doctor came again.

"You're doing very well, Alex. The medicine will ease things for you for a few days, then we'll cut you down again. I've felt, and the staff corroborates this, that you've been too hard on yourself."

And so on. It was easier to relax. Not to have to decide about Charlotte.

"Why don't you spare yourself a visitor for a few days," the doctor was saying. Just what I was thinking. "But as I understand it there was an incident with another patient that touched this off."

"Yes, I tried to kiss her," he admitted, without shame. Julia was going home soon, he remembered her saying that. She, whom he had pictured going on to another hospital, was instead going home to her parents. He was not allowed to speak to her anymore.

"The staff tells me you've been very attentive to her, that you've helped her a lot and been supportive."

"I thought she and I were going on to a state hospital. Frankly."

"Well I'm releasing Julia next week, and I doubt very much if you'll be here even the three months."

"She's going so quickly . . ."

"She responded very well. And you, Alex, I believe you'll do better a great deal faster now."

Why? But he knew why. He told the doctor about the Temporarily Out of Service sign. The doctor smiled. He smiled. A young, formal young resident, careful with his smiles. My smiling friend the doctor. Alex had only to admit to the accuracy of that sign for the time being. It was a great relief.

"Can I at least talk to Julia? I won't bother her."

"Yes of course talk to her. She's been asking about you."

Alex stayed in his room all day. In the evening he went down the hall for his six-o'clock medicine. Through the lounge door he saw Nino sitting sideways on a wooden chair talking to Julia, his calm face breaking into and falling away from smiles. They were talking together happily. Alex approached them. Julie Julie my love. Her joyful smile and serene eyes again seemed to focus on something beside him; she looked embarrassed and pleased; her hair was up in its dark heavy bun, as he had told her to wear it. He had not seen her for two days and her beauty bloomed under his eyes. He knew he had done her no harm, he looked down guiltlessly into her face. From across the room Mr. Berne strolled up, and Julia addressed him: "I no like Alex. He a trouble to me." But with joy Alex knew this was not so; it was teasing, without blame. Alex went across the lounge and sat with Michele.

"Glad to see you among the living," she said.

"Sometimes I feel like her brother."

"We're not at all alike."

"Not you. Julia."

"Why is that?"

"She says nothing superfluous, is nothing superfluous. If I could be like that . . ." He saw that Michele's face was registering disappointment that it was not her he considered his sister. "Let's play cards, Michele. I'm glad to see you again. You're my friend, you know."

They were far into a card game when Mr. Berne sat down with them.

"You'll be careful about bothering Julia, Alex?"

"She's not afraid of me," he said calmly.

Half an hour later, sitting between Mr. Berne and Alex, smiling secretly at the card game, Julia, her legs crossed neatly, the blue and green beads shining in the light, her head bent happily forward as she watched Michele shuffling the cards, Julia took Alex's hand on the edge of the table.

It was the day for Julia to go home. She was waiting for her parents to come for her. Through the open, slanted windows in the lounge Alex was watching a fine rain collecting on the screen. (We'll be talking about your discharge soon, Alex, said the doctor. I'll be glad to have you home again, Charlotte said without urgency. Nino congratulated him for being so well as they sat side by side on Nino's bed, deep in their argument about women. Alex had been allowed to take walks by himself and had come back the first time with ten copies of *The New York Times* bought at ten newsstands. That was his own private victory and no one laughed at him for it. You'll miss Julia, won't you, Miss Bergholz said gently. I'll miss you when I leave, he answered.) The day was slow and like a holiday, with the misting rain drifting over the streets; no roof today as he could not play badminton in the sun with Michele. Julia was walking around saying good-bye to everyone. He watched the door and saw her parents arrive, saw her father carrying a suitcase toward the elevators. Alex sat without impatience until Julia came up to him and they walked together into the hall where she put down her black purse and kissed his cheek.

"Do you forgive me for everything, Julia?"

"Yes," with an embarrassed open and beautiful smile. "You send me a birthday card?"

"Yes, I'll remember. September third."

"You no be here forever," she said suddenly, and they were the first words of that kind she had ever said to him. They shook hands.

Her parents preceded her through the door to the elevators while Alex stood by. "Good-bye, Mrs. Alberti," she waved, and turned toward the door. Alex felt as though someone had just floated him.

Julia picked up her bag, looked back over her shoulder at Alex, and, with her blissful smile, was gone.

The Expectancy of My Survival

I know when my mother calls me and talks in her offhand voice as though she doesn't care whether I listen or not that she has something on her mind, and so, that February morning, I said in an equally offhand voice that I'd been thinking of stopping by to see her and how about today. Fine. And then, the only sign of apprehension, she said briskly: "Around five o'clock, Jamie?" meaning five o'clock sharp, and I consented.

Actually it was inconvenient to be there by five, as it meant leaving work in Harlem early to get downtown in the rush-hour traffic. But I had learned more or less scrupulously to take her appeals in earnest. Her way may always have been the same, but I first learned it when she called me one weekend while I was sleeping over at a friend's; I was eleven and we lived then in Boston. My mother called me in the afternoon, though she was not a pestering woman and her call was unusual. She said, maybe I'd like to come home that afternoon instead of to-morrow, and somehow I took that as an order, though as I say this was the first time I noticed her method. I rode the bus home, and then my mother said would I like to go out with her to do some shopping. We walked on Charles Street among Saturday shoppers loaded with supermarket bags and my mother said: "You know how sick Jakie was?" Yes, I said with guilt, for I hadn't been to see him in the hospital, though he was my best friend. "Well he died," she said, and her arm paused but did not hold me round the shoulders. That was a stroke of genius, for something came up between me and the sidewalk; any other emotion or any touch to distract me from it was repellent. "He died this noon, very quietly, Jamie. I know what good friends you were, but you mustn't be too sorry. It would make Jakie happier if you go right on . . ." Playing. But I had stolen Jakie's marbles last week and that was why I had been ashamed to face him sick. We were like twin brothers because our names were alike, and we bought identical winter coats, tan, with fuzzy linings. Then my mother deflected me into a store and we bought fruit and vegetables, and the first brutal episode of my life was over.

There have been small and large crises since then and I always know by her voice on the phone to make it over there fast. I am very accommodating to my mother, since she has no husband now and only a daughter who lives in Boston; so I am the man in her life, and for all I know she is the woman in mine.

My mother always wanted me to be a musician. It started off with her wanting it because I wanted it; we were living in Boston when I was eight and I went to a small private school where I was the only kid who couldn't play an instrument or speak French. Those kids were years ahead of me—I came from the back woods of Maine —and I was given a triangle to play in the class orchestra. I played it with arrogant pride, became in fact an expert on the various tones one can ring out of that ridiculous instrument. And then I began piano lessons. My teacher was an old maid who lived in a stone house on Beacon Hill. I pushed the doorbell which rang off in the recesses of high stone rooms and I waited looking through the grilled door and hearing the dog yapping till I saw Miss Holmes sweeping down a spiral staircase. The rooms were so big that the furniture was oversized: a hall table big enough for a banquet, and a sofa that could have slept six. Along the way through the rooms were huge bowls full of nuts and candy that went stale before the dishes could be eaten empty by myself and other children who nibbled their way along behind Miss Holmes to the practice room upstairs. My mother bought me a little plastic imitation-leather briefcase for my music books and I carried it manfully with professional feeling. Finally I played in one of Miss Holmes's afternoons for parents, I played Mozart and Bach while the mothers and fathers sat in the dark with their heads cocked. At home I practiced violently by the hour; my mother saw me as a true genius, but I practiced to keep away from my homework. It was the first time she did not mind my bad grades, for she saw me in her mind always as she had seen me in a little suit playing Bach in front of all the parents; there she had seen me in the flesh excelling, and how did she know what I looked like sweating over a history test or delivering French memorized passages in class? Once a parent has seen you performing and you are no longer an abstraction who stays away all day at school, you've had it. From then on it was my mother who wanted me to be a musician, long after I had lost interest and only played to keep away from history.

I kept it up in deference to her, studying music theory and conducting in college. But by then something else had entered my mind, and after college I went to teach kids in Harlem. I have a piano at home and some friends from Juilliard who come and we play together. Also I have a slant on getting to the children I teach. Everyone has his own: one girl I know takes them to the park and they watch birds and the coming and going of leaves in various seasons; another guy has them all writing autobiographies; and I have them listening to music. I take a portable phonograph to class and the kids and I listen. We listen to Bach and we listen to jazz. So far this year I've gotten them to understand the mechanics of a fugue, and as for jazz they can tell me more than I can tell them; but this makes them see that music is music whether it's classical or not. And then I brought them a record of the Beatles baroque music and the jazz-Bach, and one of Leontyne Price singing and I passed around the jacket with the picture of her big and black and famous, and recently they've wanted me to take them to a concert and I'll do it.

I got to East Sixtieth Street soon after five. My mother no longer lives in the Village; she has moved up in the world and it suits her fine. It's a long way from Concord, Mass., to Chicago to Maine to Boston to East Sixtieth Street. She is now an editor on a woman's magazine, good money and a lousy publication; she's the kind of woman who likes Jane Austen and Henry James. It was nearly dark that February afternoon as I walked up her street passing the girls on their way to Bloomingdale's and the executives returning home with their real leather briefcases. These girls are not my dish. Self-consciously chic, handing over their small pay checks for the bargains of Bloomingdale's, they buy their clothes straight out of the *Times* ads—the burden of the world to dress well in this city which, so less guileless girls tell me, is full of married men and fags. I think of my sister Jenny who has other burdens and at least her shoulders are less bony. But perhaps she has her own way of hunting a man.

Inside my mother's door I got the abrupt news. The offhand manner is dispatched with now that I've arrived.

"Jenny's quit college."

"At this time of year?"

"Try to be sensible. She's not. She quit when she felt like it. Do you think a thing like tuition would stop her? Jamie, make yourself a drink. You'll have to go see her."

Hearing myself called Jamie, as I have been called Jim by everyone away from home, reminds me that we are Jamie and Jenny, very cute, and that we were cute kids together, admired on buses and by other parents, not for our alliterative names but for our twinlike natures. We aren't twins but we were more like twins than twins themselves. We faced the world like two little soldiers, I in my crew cut and she in her helmet hair. Since then we have gone our various ways but there are little clots of blood that beat up in my arms when I know Jenny is in trouble. For a moment her blood is in my vessels and I panic for her.

I sat with my drink and we talked it over. My mother is no great believer in education, not per se, but for Jenny it's an institution to keep her out of trouble. If she quits college, then there is trouble like an abyss into which she'll fly willingly. My sister's been through it all—abortion, hospital emergency rooms, and several psychiatrists with whom she became aggressive; she quit them too. Trouble curves over the surface of her world and going to college is like entering the force of gravity; now she has soared off, out of the earth's atmosphere into the upper regions of calamity. That's how my mother saw it and I tended to agree. All right, I'll go to Boston this weekend.

She won't have missed enough classes that she can't go back in.

Then we talked about me. I told my mother I was going to take my kids to a concert but I hadn't decided which one yet. She veered the conversation to the concert side and asked me how my musical evenings with my Juilliard friends were going. Secretly she hopes they will break down the barriers for me and get me to play in Philharmonic Hall. So I let her think it. I was never as excited about the fugue myself as I was excited to have gotten it across to my kids. But her mind goes where it wants and why should a boy of twenty-one tell a woman of forty-nine what to think?

When I was all ready to leave, the talk swung back to Jenny and my mother said in an offhand voice: "She wants to go out and visit your father and I don't think that's a good idea for her." So this was the crisis, and not Jenny's quitting. If she is free of college she can go live with our father. Worse trouble than the upper regions of calamity. My mother isn't what you'd call generous in her appraisal of her ex-husband. I let this piece of information take hold as I said good-bye and promised to do all I could. But I had an uneasy realization that Jenny has taken one more tack away from me and that I am inadequate to follow the reasons. I couldn't even remember the last time she and I talked about our father.

I have been called in on other crises concerning Jenny and they are all the same. Her flying trip to Puerto Rico for an abortion. Her turning herself into a Boston hospital emergency room for shooting up too much heroin. The night she ran naked in the street. And every time I go to Boston as though my suitcase were empty and I am taking nothing with me to deal with her. And it's not as though

93

my mother is shocked at anything Jenny does; she has an unusually generous nature toward her daughter, and even agreed with the doctors that it was better for Jenny to live in another city from her mother. It's as though my mother accepts with wide-eyed wonder that she herself might be the cause of Jenny's difficulty. With no more guilt than if she had given birth to a cripple. And like the messenger from her heart I go out to rescue Jenny and set her back on her feet away from the disastrous influence of her mother.

That night I had a date for dinner with my present girl friend, Alfrieda. Rather a heavy name for a pretty little thing like that. But she likes to be called Alfrieda, not Didi as she was called as a child, as though the bigness of her name will pole her into womanhood. She is still very young and I admire the leaps and bounds with which she enters the grown-up world. We had an interesting talk once about our names: how I was Jim to the world and Jamie to my mother, how she was Alfrieda to the world and Didi to her parents. We felt like conspirators in the outside air and that night I fell in love with her. I have been in love since I was fifteen, with one girl or another, so I can't say that the occurrence overwhelmed me. But Alfrieda was my first girl with a grown-up name; they were all Patty and Ellie and Muff before that. True to their mothers' hearts. Alfrieda was a real winner.

That night I told her I was going to Boston for Jenny. I hadn't known Alfrieda long so she had no idea about Jenny except that she went to Boston University. It was Ellie who went through the abortion crisis with me, very impressed by the melodramatics in my family. When I told Alfrieda Jenny had quit college, she said: "What a terrible thing to do. She'll be sorry later." And then remembering to be grown-up she added: "But college isn't everything of course. She's interested in painting isn't she?" Alfrieda goes to Barnard and wouldn't stop for the world. "My parents would never give me money if I left," she once confided in me; "and you can't get a job without a degree. I know because I read the *Times* want ads and they always say college graduate, all the interesting jobs anyway." But my Alfrieda at least doesn't get a pay check, neither does she look at those other ads in the *Times,* the clothes ads, and when she has pocket money to spend she spends it on books and food and splitting the check with me for dinner or a play. That makes her feel grown-up too, like an independent woman. She seems to have a notion that because I work in Harlem I'm poor too, and when I pay for dinner she reads the price side of the menu before the chicken and beef side. And Alfrieda likes to eat; she eats all her potatoes and orders a cheap gooey dessert. This little girl appeals to me; she has not yet entered the man hunt, and perhaps she will fall into the arms of a man without knowing the hunt exists. She reminds me of the fresh-cheeked girls in Maine, the junior high school girls when I was in the third grade, who liked to play girls' basketball and had sleep-overs on weekends. They smelled sweaty as they came out of the gym, and after their weekends they looked blissfully tired and conspiratorial; it was only after they went to dances with the boys that they looked just plain exhausted. Alfrieda looks like that, set in another class. I do not want to harm her although I exhaust her and will not be the man in whose arms she will escape the hunt. That night I took her back to her dormitory solemnly and said I'd call when I got back to the city. She did not know the source of my solemnity and believed it to be the catastrophic matters on my mind concerning Jenny. With equal solemnity she did not even kiss me good-bye.

I took the shuttle plane to Boston on Saturday morning, though I prefer the train, but the weekend was short. I prefer trains because then I can think and see the world go the way I think it must go but would feel like a maniac letting myself see it that way every day on my way to work. More about the world later. That day on the plane I thought about our father; it was like cramming for an exam to be ready for Jenny. I haven't seen my father since I was ten, but I remember him as a heavy-faced man with handsome features and big limbs. He's a stockbroker in Chicago. My mother divorced him when I was two and Jenny just born, and she took us to Maine where she had a divorcée woman-friend and where she got a job on a Down East magazine of which she eventually became editor. But this is not about my father. How can I know about him when all those years were lived in spite of him? He paid his alimony on time, for which my mother gave him due credit, and otherwise she only said obliquely that he was a selfish man. Her favorite story to point this up is that on her birthday the second year they were married he *had* to go to New York on business and forgot to call her to wish her many happy returns. They didn't have many more happy returns together. Jenny and I made periodic trips to New York when we were living in Boston and Daddy came to New York on business. He never took us kite-flying in Central Park, though I saw children with Chinese fish and bird kites there which gave me my first romance for New York City. Instead we stayed in a big fancy carpeted hotel which only brought out the latent stiffness one feels with an absent father, and we went to the Statue of Liberty, and to the Empire State Building in a taxi. We passed the double-decker buses on Fifth Avenue and I wished I had a father who would think of taking us on those. The last time I saw him, eleven years ago, was just before his second marriage. He tried to talk man to man with me and I stiffly refused. As for Jenny, she was just the little soldier at my side, the little girl my father remembered to take to the bathroom, and who gave me someone else to accuse besides myself of being formal and awkward. So what does she remember that makes her want to go to Chicago? Unless it's that she prefers taxis and sees him as the perfect daddy.

Perfect perhaps because he's Jewish, and Jenny occasionally feels very Jewish. It's her way of charging her mother, her excuse for having nothing to say to her mother. For what does a Jew have to say to Eleanor Ames Wolf from Concord, Mass.? But Jenny's half-Jewishness, like my own, is an abstract quality, since we grew up with Eleanor Ames Wolf. This abstract Jewishness only confirms Jenny's picture of herself as a noble but semifreak in an Anglo-Saxon world. But irony of ironies, our father, who gave us our half-Jewish blood, makes, for some reason known only to himself, a great show of *not* being Jewish. As though having brushed up against our mother and his second wife he has absorbed their Anglo-Saxon preferences and customs. He celebrates Christmas with a flourish, mails us presents wrapped by his own thick fingers, beautifully, but with mashed ribbon. Does Jenny hope to go to him so that Jennifer Ames Wolf and Tommy Wolf can pool their partial but mutual Jewishness and become—a Jewish family?

As for my mother, if she feels guiltless about her crippled daughter, you can be sure she finds our father the guilty one, all by himself, even in absentia.

All this occupied me till Boston for the mind strays into

details, remembering the kind of shoes my father wore, and it takes longer to think than to tell. I went straight to Jenny's apartment out on Marlborough Street. There was her name on the mailbox: Jennifer Wolf. She knew girls should only put their first initial on their bells and so conceal their sex, but that was just like Jenny—asking trouble to ring her doorbell.

Upstairs she opened the door and said: "Hello, Jim," as though I lived right around the corner, and she gave me an offhand kiss on the cheek; in spite of the psychiatrists she retains some of her mother's habits.

"Come on in. I'm painting this table over so you'll have to watch, unless you want a brush."

"Well I don't."

"Okay, be your usual piggish self," she said, and went right on painting her table wagon blue.

I sat in an uncomfortable wooden chair and lit a cigarette casually.

"I guess Mother sent you up here," she said, dabbing in the center of the table.

"Sure she did. Did you think I was an ambassador of good will all by myself?"

Jenny gave me a lively appreciative glance and waved the brush in a way her fastidious mother would have hated to see. Blue specks of paint flew around the room, landing like summer flies on the sofa and walls. One settled on Jenny's cheek.

"I'm in trouble, Jim. I don't especially want to see her representative."

"Okay. Let's say she sent me but I'm not necessarily representing her."

"Damn you, Jim, can't you ever do anything she wouldn't do?"

I wagged my head foolishly, as though considering. One

way or another I would force her to stop being offhand. Her voice was already dropping down into various registers of seriousness.

"Jim, I'm in trouble," she said, in a different voice than she had said it earlier. Her brushing hand steadied along the table, layering blue like milk over the surface. "I told my biology professor he was reactionary, and walked out."

"Nothing wrong with that, if it's accurate."

"But he hadn't said anything for an hour. We were in lab. I just stood up and said it. Then I sold all my books and told my adviser I was quitting. That's not so serious, Jim, I know that. But I can't get a fix on what I want to say. Will you remind me?"

"About your being in trouble?"

"Oh yes. Trouble. Jim, every day I walk around the buildings at B.U. trying to want to walk back in. It all looks so nice, you know, Jim? The boys are all wearing those duffer coats with leather buttons and carrying their books in their arms. You'd think their books were little babies. It's so—it's so *sweet*, Jim. I stand there and feel like crying, and I think what nice husbands they'd make. And—where was I?"

"Wanting to walk back in."

"Yes. So I walk around and then I get sick. All over. I feel like I'm going to throw up. So I can't go into school like that, can I? I have to come home in case I throw up, don't I?"

"Frankly I think you should stay out of college and get a job like everybody else."

"I'm not like everybody else."

"No, you're a scared rabbit, but if you went and got a job you might find the world is made up of other scared rabbits and you might find yourself a member of the human race."

This was not what I had intended to say. Suddenly I am feeling a little Jewish myself. Which only means, for me, that I have been harboring astonishment at my mother's deviousness, which for lack of a better adjective I label Anglo-Saxon. I looked at Jenny, at her shiny pale eyes that seem to register the molecules swarming in from all directions and to flinch back from them. I don't, at this moment, want her to behave like her mother's good little B.U. student.

"If you want to get a job I'm all for it. I don't care how scared you . . ."

Swiftly Jenny flung her arms around my neck and kissed me on the head.

"What I like about you is you're a real dope," she said and went back to work leaving a spot of blue paint on my shirt.

"So where shall I get a job?"

"I don't know. What can you do? Type? Go to the Fine Arts Museum. Can you wait on tables? Sing and dance? Honestly, Jen, you're hopeless, asking me where to look. Buy the paper, read the want ads." I thought of Alfrieda who was spared all this and had entered the ranks of human beings long ago and without effort. "Unless you want to go back to school. They'll still take you."

"I didn't take my mid-year exams."

"You could make them up. Give the professors a sad story and break their hearts."

"I'm sick of breaking hearts to get what I want. Poor Jennifer Wolf, let's give her a break 'cause she's sick in the head."

"Are you seeing a doctor?"

"Yes."

"What does he say?"

"To see him more often and get plenty of sleep. One day I'll wake up at the end of the rainbow and shrunk to half my size."

"How does he shrink you?"

"On the couch and it's a damn uncomfortable one too. Finally I brought my own pillow. Do you know what he has, Jim? He has a little clean napkin on the back of the couch and I get so stiff in the neck I can't think. Anyway it's more of the same."

"What is?"

"Staring at the wall and talking into space, just like being at home only with him I have to speak up. I don't even know if my words get to him, they're printed all over the walls. It's like home movies." She put a finishing splotch of blue and neatened it up. "Jim, I've been reading Greek philosophers."

"What for?"

"They had to start from scratch too. Let me read you something nice."

She picked up a book which was spine-broken by the sofa and sat down and read: " 'The following were his watchwords and precepts; don't step over the beam of balance, don't sit down on your bushel, don't eat your heart, don't commit a nuisance towards the sun. . . . This is what they meant: Don't step over the beam of balance: don't overstep the bounds of equity and justice. Don't sit down on your bushel: have the same care of to-day and the future, a bushel being the day's ration. By not eating your heart he meant not wasting your life in troubles and pains.' " She shut the book. "That's Diogenes talking about Pythagoras. Only he doesn't interpret all the precepts, like the one about being a nuisance toward the sun and that's my favorite."

It's just like Jenny to skip over all that other good advice for a poetical concept she couldn't grasp.

"Are you going to stay till tomorrow?" Jenny asked indifferently.

"Yes."

"Is that time enough to convert me to your mother's way of thinking?"

"She's your mother too. And what's all this about going out to see Dad?"

"Daddy wrote me a sweet letter and invited me out. We have half brothers and sisters you know, half of our flesh and blood. Or did you think you sprang from your mother all by yourself?"

"Don't be vile. I think it's a good idea. Why don't you go?"

"Well it's a starting point. But it's not a job."

"You could get a job out there."

"I can't start that much from scratch," she said, using the expression for the second time. It's funny how people can't forget the central issue even in conversation. She was obsessed by a phrase which summed up her predicament and which even her good ear did not censor out, although she never repeated herself otherwise. It was like a little pebble in watery sentences.

"It's another kind of starting point. You might get to know Dad. They're important, you know, fathers," I said judiciously.

"How should you know?"

"I'd like to get to know him too but I have a job."

"Oh my human brother. Do you want to come with me?"

"No. I said I have a job. Look, Jenny, either you go back to school or you get a job here or you go to Chicago. Three possibilities. Like, shall I have beef, fish, or chicken." Alfrieda again, but the price to pay was not important to Jenny. "So you try to know which will taste best, which idea of taste appeals to you, and then you say: beef."

"Fish," said Jenny.

"So then you say to yourself, having chosen fish, do I now wish it were beef or am I happy with fish, having said it. You try out a decision and if you're sorry you know you chose wrong, so try again. Out of the three choices it won't take long. You can't do this abstractly, you make the choice and see how it rests with you. Okay? Now, what do you want to do?"

"Stay in school."

"How does it feel now you've said it?"

"Awful. I really wanted a job."

"Great. The field is narrowing. How does it feel, wanting a job?"

"Terrible. I'll go to Chicago."

"Then that's it. Out you go."

"No that isn't it."

"Why not?"

"I feel awful about that too and I don't want it."

I lit another cigarette without surprise or disappointment. I should have known that given three possibilities she would need a fourth. So I gave up the conversation for that day and we talked of other things; I hoped to see something accidentally so that after all it would turn out that I had just the right thing for her in my empty suitcase.

That night I had the chance to see how the world could go, and I lay in the blankets on the sofa stiff with sleeplessness and saw it go. Think about mass and space. But right off the surface of the table there is space. The table might not exist; it's only bunched molecules. Think of containers of fluid: honey in jars, milk or gin in bottles, bottles of ink. This is not chemical but mechanical solidification; not like bread or a candy bar. Suppose all those things weren't contained, everyone's house a flood of honey and ink. So small is the line between order and chaos. Funny that people who are just a mass of cells and the accident of just that sperm piercing that egg rather than another sperm and egg should take life so seriously. Why do they paint that table blue or put that sofa there against the wall, and why do they marry that person so carefully and have a whole following sweep of episodes that constitutes life and habit? Why not marry anyone, another collection of cells like oneself? But if you thought like this too much you wouldn't do a thing—a crippling of the will. One bothers to paint a table because goddammit I'll live forever. Or for a year. It is all an effort to forget the accident and to take a stand against dying; even for a year it's worth it. A future is contained in the buying of a particular sofa and the painting of a table . . . But as I see it one could take away the bottle around the ink. Take away the force holding together the molecules in a table. Take away the skin that hides the systems of the body and which makes up what we call beauty. And what do you have left? and that could be done. You would see life as it really is, quivering with atoms, and I have seen it go that way often. You can't take away the earth's spin or the seasons, but all the rest is our stab to defy that turning of the earth and the line of evolution. Here we are in spite of an expanding universe and even if we are only a step to something higher, here we are and we'll put our foot down, together . . . Everything in containers . . . Only I lose the sense of it, I stare and see the walls dissolve and then I feel calm. My grip is relaxed and I touch the world at all points; its chaos equals my own. I thrashed around on the small sofa my sister had bothered to buy for herself, and then I slept.

Jenny clattering cups in the kitchenette woke me up to the same old world.

Jenny poured me coffee and we sat at the newly painted table which was dry and fresh as a Dutch painting. In her most beside-the-point manner she said:

"Jim, I'm going to get a job. I decided last night, and then I was glad. It was fish all along."

"What about Chicago?"

"Daddy? Yes, I'd get to know him. But so what. Fathers are accidents, like something *given* in geometry. I was never good at geometry. I can't prove anything. Someday, Jim, when I feel I have a past. Right now I'm a balloon." Jenny sees the world go just the way I do, and astonished frightened blood clotted in my wrists. "And I'd like to get a job and . . . well, you said it, I didn't, meet the human race. Only, Jim . . ."

"Yes," I said, stirring the coffee which was burnt and knowing she was no more offhand.

"Jim, when I get a job I'll call you up and tell you what it is and where it is and exactly what I have to do, and will you stick by me? I'm not sitting down on my bushel goddammit," she cried suddenly, making a grab for my arm. "Will you call me up and write?"

"Sure I will Jenny."

"I'll buy the paper. What do I do? I go around and say: this is me, I'm just starting from scratch—but I can't say that can I?"

"You say: here I am and I'm as good as the next one."

"Do you think I'm as good as the next one?"

"Easily."

"But I never did anything lately without making that excuse, you know, I'm sick and all, give me a break."

"You don't need a break. Just ask for the job and if they don't give it to you, ask for another."

"But what about Mother? She'd want me to get oh such a special job, the best."

"Forget Mother. She wants you on your feet so she can come and take you in her arms."

"She wanted college and summa cum laude."

"She'll get what she gets, Jenny. Let's stick to you."

A great hurdle had been cleared and it was all words after that. I knew that I might have to come to Boston again, that she'd take a job and quit and swallow a handful of pills or smoke herself into oblivion on hash, that this new three-dimensional world was more the hope of height than the attainment of it. But I couldn't let her see the faltering in me lest she see it in herself. We went out and bought the Boston *Globe* and made a list of phone numbers from the classified section, and then it was time to whisk off to the airport. I got a taxi at the corner of the Public Gardens and I saw Jenny standing hunched in the cold waving me off to my human world while she let go of the force of gravity and went up into possible calamity. She lit a cigarette in the frosty air and I saw her as the taxi rounded the park blowing breath and smoke around her face and waving like a tough orphan on a street corner.

I was puttering around in my apartment picking out records for tomorrow's classes when my mother called. But nothing offhand about it.

"Jamie, Jennifer called tonight and she tells me she's not going back to college."

"That's right."

"And why isn't she going to Chicago, if I may ask?"

"That's . . . that's really starting from scratch," I said, picking up Jenny's pebble. "She'll go someday to visit, it'd be good for her. But she needs to start up on home territory."

"And I take it you were instrumental in persuading her to want to work instead of finishing school."

"She's all right. She's reading Greek philosophy."

"Don't be flippant, Jamie. This is crucial." She asks me to be a man and calls me by my boy's name; but these are the least of a parent's inconsistencies.

"Look, Mother, she doesn't need school. She has a good head and she needs to find out she's human like anybody else."

"She's not human. She's a very sick girl and she should stay out of trouble."

"She can't stay in school forever. You've got to trust the timing of her quitting now. She wants . . . she wants . . . she sees a way out."

"A way out of what?"

"Out of the need to say: I'm sick. Let her out. She'll fall on her face a few times but she'll be trying. In school she can only think she can't even try."

Then suddenly I realized that this situation was unique. There had been no doubt that Jenny had to have an abortion, or had to be bailed out of the emergency room, and I had to be there just to hold her hand. This time I had brought my judgment to bear and I had helped to keep her out of Boston University. This was no hard and fast law that Jenny had to follow for her own good; this was choice, and we had chosen against our mother. Suddenly I felt like a kid again side by side with my helmet-haired sister defying our mother: that our father was *not* selfish, that we would *not* go to Sunday school. And I saw Jenny run from the house away from Mother's voice and go charging down the street with her helmet-head lowered like a G.I. entering combat.

Then I heard my mother's voice go cold. "Well I'm disappointed in you, Jamie. I thought you were a sensible boy and would help her. What she needs is the confinement of an institution till she finds herself. I've gone on thinking you were a solid boy, devoted to your talent but with a genius for helping others, as you're helping those children in Harlem, by sharing the thing you love most. I didn't expect you to guide your sister the wrong way like this. I sent you to help her, to get her back to college . . ."

"Mother, I went by myself. Nobody sent me."

There was a small silence filled with meaning. Then: "Well you can be sure I won't ask you again. I hope you won't disappoint me the way she has."

And I bit my tongue to keep from saying: she can't disappoint you, you can't expect anything, she's sick. So well do these concepts stick in our guts.

We said good-bye formally. And I called Alfrieda at the dorm. It was late and her voice came dull with sleep. But I pictured her pink and drowsy, innocent and a born member of the human race.

"Oh hello, Jim. How was your trip?"

"Swell. I did what I had to do. I helped my sister get a job."

"I thought you wanted her to go back to college."

"No."

"Well I missed you. My parents want you to come to dinner this week. Will you come?"

"I'll come," I said as though speaking from the moon. I felt a kind of appalling distaste for this human girl but a need to be in her presence. As though she were a promise of the other possibilities that the sperm and the egg had. A unique combination. We said good-bye after assorted plans for the week.

The next day we discussed in class where to go hear some music, and we decided on the opera. It would set me back a bit to take all my kids to the opera, but they liked the idea of the back row of the top balcony especially when I told them you get dizzy up there.

So in the late afternoon I walked around with my hands in my pockets in the unfamiliar streets of Harlem. They were unfamiliar but I felt at home there, as though my strangeness were emerging and being noticed. The blacks are no more surprised at my strangeness than I am. To be white among the blacks, to have at least one peculiarity recognized on the spot, rests easier than to be white among the whites and have the eccentricities tucked away like an internal disorder. My friends and I would have a musical evening at home that night and that was fine with me. But had I ever really wanted to be a musician? Not really. I was years too late anyway; the boys I knew at Juilliard had had their first public performance. But sometimes I saw myself in a black suit over the keyboard on a stage, and the picture buoyed me up: a tangible possibility to be in the eyes of the world the little boy growing up in the eyes of his mother. That picture had floated in my head and kept me company; sometimes I thought I was a special guy as though it were an accomplished fact. But face to face with it I saw with my own eyes that I had not the talent and would never get on that stage. And the picture dissolved like another self, I felt something fall away from me that had lived there for years. And I was not sorry to see it go.

Jenny called me that night.

"Jim, I looked for jobs but I didn't get one."

"Where'd you look?"

"I went to the museum but they didn't need anyone. I went to a bookstore, and for a typing job but I can't really type well. I had to lie. I liked the bookstore best."

"There are other bookstores."

"I already thought of that. Jim, are you still there?"

"Of course I am."

"No, I mean still behind me?"

"Yes Jenny I am."

"Jim, you're a real dope," she said and hung up.

And how is the world going to go? It's going to go the same way, only we're doing a very good job of keeping things in containers. Especially on the subway I notice this, looking at the ads. What optimism, to put up an ad and expect it to form taste for at least a few months. Think of the work that goes into that printed sheet: someone to think up the ad (not to mention the businessmen behind the product), someone to do layout, then the printers print it and someone else cuts it to just the right size, and then someone has to put it in the right-sized rack. There they stand, advising me about shampoo, cigarettes, and what paper to read. With the utmost confidence that my skin will hold together and that we will be on the face of the earth in a year's turning. And such confidence of a whole rank of specialized men in the expectancy of my survival does wonders for me, every day.

The Girl Who Liked Communists

Released, Jenny ran downstairs two at a time, shedding good behavior. Outside the building, the street was empty, and winter stood a still blue behind the city. A Saturday afternoon, in Boston, in a January freeze, 1952. The girl set off aimlessly; she was stooped to one side from carrying a bookbag over her right shoulder during the weekdays. Two blue diffident eyes fixed themselves on the sidewalk a foot ahead as she walked; there was a smear of ink near her mouth. She had an hour to kill before meeting her friend Karen, and she would kill it in the stores across the Common, stealing. She headed in that direction, but slowly, to get in the mood. Upstairs in the apartment, practicing the piano, dutifully answering her mother's questions—yes, she'd done her geography, no this was Mozart not Bach, and sorry she couldn't help banging the keys she hated the piano—she had kicked a raw spot on the back of her heel with the toe of the other foot: the agony of not being herself. Outdoors her grim little mouth parted, she sucked at the cold air; the real world was about to be entered, where she was happiest and alone. She jaywalked across Beacon Street and suddenly pulled her lips together and whistled a song. She was getting in the mood.

She always hated to be seen walking with her mother, a good girl in her blue coat with gold sailor buttons. Today, wearing an old short brown coat with a hood, she strolled boldly, hands in pockets, fastening her eyes on everyone as she passed. Gritted snow was left clotted under trees in the Common; old people sat on the benches with arms wrapped around their rib cages. Jenny watched two soldiers approaching until one of them said: "Well, hello there," and then she averted her eyes cautiously. She liked the bums particularly, each one occupying a bench by himself. One of them with a paper package in his lap gave her a small rotten smile like a man who has just thrown up. She smiled back as though he were her best friend. Then she dodged a family, a father and mother and boy, and the mood was solidified: the little boy shot a sly admiring look at her as she strolled by, her hands in her pockets and her chin lifted; her eyes skimmed off his face; at eleven she strolled all by herself. Now she was ready and walked faster. The afternoon promised much and with a nervous hand pushing her hair off her face she trotted across the street toward the dime store.

She was good at this. She made for the toy counter and inspected toy soldiers until, nobody looking, she pocketed one: a soldier on his belly with a gun. The woman behind the counter came her way. "Yes dear, may I help you?" A flush of alarm spread in Jenny's head: she had just noticed a soldier with a gun over his shoulder, nonchalant, breezy, with a perfect plastic nose. That was the one she wanted. She turned an innocent smile up to the woman. "No thanks. My kid brother might like one of these but I don't know which one." Not that she had a kid brother. But the idea gripped her. She had her older brother Jamie, for whom she had never been able to do anything. Jenny turned over a few soldiers appraisingly, considering which one would appeal to the kid brother. Decidedly it was the man with the gun over his shoulder. She moved along the counter. Out of range of the woman she inspected key chains with little dogs hanging on them; swiftly she pocketed a handful. Red or blue dogs. Useless. She craved that soldier. But she had hung around the toy counter too long so she strolled over to the candy counter and gathered up some chocolate drops in silver paper, a candy bar, and some gum. All useless. Then she went off into the corner and looked at lamp shades. No one would suspect her here, you can't pocket a lamp shade. She ran her hands over them, turned them, thinking of the soldier. He had such a nice beaked perfect nose; he stood casually; war was a great joy to him, like walking out in the woods. Purposefully as though to leave the store Jenny passed by the toy counter and saw the soldier of her choice tossed on his side in a heap of plastic men, his jaunty head pressed against by another soldier's booted foot. Swiftly she stood him upright under the eyes of the woman behind the counter. "Have you made up your mind?" the woman asked. "No I can't. Could you tell me what time it is?" "It's just three." "I have to go," Jenny said. Time to meet Karen. She left the store. Nothing like this had ever happened. Not once had she desired anything that went into her pocket, or failed to get into her pocket.

She was late and ran kitty corner across the Common to the Public Gardens. Karen was standing against a tree. Jenny pushed her hand through her hair, shoved it behind her ears; she was not in the mood for Karen any more. Before trotting across the street she threw the soldier who lay on his belly into a trash barrel. The trees in the Gardens stood huge and bare like the skeletons of mammoth animals, that in the summer would be sleek and fat with leaves. For the first time that day she felt chilled. She crossed the street and said Hi to Karen, pulled out a silver-wrapped chocolate and offered it. The two girls' eyes took each other in. They were supposed to look alike and were called sidekicks in school; the kitchen staff could not tell them apart. Each looked at the other, to see herself. Controlled eyes: the slight pride, the slight distaste one has for oneself. "What shall we do?" Jenny asked. "I want to buy some trading cards." "Okay. I know where to go." They cut through the Public Gardens, crossing the bridge with its globed lights, throwing pebbles down into the water. Jenny felt her heart break; she had left the soldier who strode along joyfully. A small pain rose in her throat, heated her brain. She had to drag herself along beside Karen, putting distance between herself and the soldier of her choice. Church spires stood up around the edges of the Gardens; her mother had told her it was a beautiful little park; she believed it; she walked through it. But she didn't like it. No bums sat on benches here. The promises as she passed by the bums in the Common and smiled at them. This park looked oppressively pretty, correct, charming; with her mother's eyes in her head she saw it. But in her own skin Jenny disliked it. The two girls left the Gardens and cut across streets to buy their trading cards. They looked very much alike.

It was always a little awkward seeing Karen outside of school. At school under other people's eyes the two girls converged on one another like twin images and canceled each other out; on the outside their differences emerged, and they hedged in the differences, and often became irritable. For Jenny it was an envious irritation, the kind of raging skin-knowledge she had when, daydreaming that she was another person altogether, she had to suddenly realize that she was still Jenny and could only be better, or spared, in her dream. That Saturday afternoon she and Karen bickered, bickered about which cards to buy, bickered back along the streets to the Public Gardens about whether to buy ice cream or not—Jenny won and they went without it—and sat on a bench at the edge of the pond bickering. Karen was talking about home, which irritated Jenny; Karen never talked about home while they were at school. The rage was arriving, the envy of Karen for her father, whom Jenny loved. How her father was building her bookshelves in her room, how he had called Karen his little scholar and was giving her some of his books.

"What do you want his books for? Half of them are in German," demanded Jenny, hunched over and raging, the sweat coming out across her back.

"Someday I'll be able to read them. I'm going to take German in high school."

"German's ugly. The Germans are rotten people."

"Oh the *Germans!* Who's talking about the Germans? But Pop says I should read some of their stuff when I'm older, like Freud and Marx . . ."

"Marx," whispered Jenny. Karen's father wore pink-rimmed glasses (Army benefits he said) and kissed Jenny on the forehead like a priest when she went to visit. He smiled a lot at her and called her Jenny Marx. "Jenny Marx, maybe you'll grow up to be a Jenny Marx," he smiled. But his eyes were steady and serious above the smile, as though smiling had never gotten that far up his face. The lenses of his pink-rimmed glasses flashed, then went clear again revealing the sunken gray eyes like two gray-streaked windowpanes. "How's my other daughter?" he would say, smiling and looking at Jenny and Karen in mock confusion. "Can I tell which of you is my real daughter?" His chapped bony hands were lined black over the knuckles with grease and he smoked with the cigarette half into his mouth, spitting out the loose shreds of tobacco.

Jenny produced the stolen candy bar and broke it in half. She was feeling sick, and sweating, and she ate her half with a vengeance, sickness against sickness, her stomach rising to receive new sickness. Her own father was never mentioned; only occasionally her mother referred to his aging fat, his talent with stocks (referred to with mockery), and how Jews were supposed to be strong on families and wasn't he a fine Jew ignoring his children. He doesn't *ignore* us, cried Jenny, he sends us Christmas presents. He's busy, he lives too far away, Jamie said. But her mother said Jew in a special voice, her Concord, Mass., voice as Jamie said. Jenny's face in the mirror was more like her mother's: small, small-featured, pale eyes and lank hair, an Anglo-Saxon face—Anglo-Saxon, that was a word she had always known. She inspected her face in the mirror until she found a thick spread at the top of the nose. "Mother," she said, "I have a Jewish nose." And her mother told her that Anglo-Saxons have noses like that too, that her own father's nose looked like Jenny's; she must have gotten her nose from Grandpa Ames. "But I'm Jenny Wolf, not Ames," said Jenny, fingering her nose. "Well your name is Wolf but you really are an Ames," said her mother, Eleanor Ames Wolf. Jennifer Ames Wolf. JAW. And James Alden Wolf. JAW. It wasn't particularly funny. She and Jamie could have just been JW; that Anglo-Saxon middle-name insertion only made it ridiculous. Her mother's assertion that they were really Anglo-Saxon.

"By the way," Karen said. "I forgot to tell you something." Karen always "forgot to tell" the most important things; a little rise of hope drew Jenny up on the bench. In an expectation of resurrected happiness she glanced joyfully along the pond, and across that view flashed a scattering of trading cards; Karen was throwing them into the water, and they flashed their colors and brief imagined scenes before they skittered into the pond. "I found these papers in the cellar. My mother isn't my mother at all." Jenny turned and stared at the twisted face; Karen's face twisted and she gazed after the sinking cards. "My real mother's been in a hospital. You know, an insane asylum. They were never going to tell me, I'll bet you that. Even Pop lied to me."

The two girls were sitting on a bench eating the silver-wrapped chocolates.

"I always hated my mother anyway. And now she's not my mother. My mother's in the loony bin," Karen said. Jenny flattened out a piece of silver paper and pressed it smooth against the bench with her fingernail. The rage returned, but doubled. She envied Karen her excuse for not loving her mother. Karen had no mother to love; or else her real mother was worthy of so much love. Jenny herself was one evening walking up the stairs to their apartment behind her own mother and she looked up to see the slope of shoulders gathered forward for the climb. "Don't forget to wipe your feet, Jenny." The denial of the dark snowy streets they had been walking through, in an easy silence. The bulb on the stairs shattered her mother's face as she turned on the landing to order Jenny to wipe her feet, breaking up the soft and featureless silent face and presenting Jenny with the lines of anger, her mother's anger and disappointment. Hated her mother then, her recognition of hate, the naming of a feeling that stabbed in her always through the attempt to love. How her mother forced her to be good and polite; how the flight into streets and stores freed her; how stealing was *bad,* she was bad, and happiest in it.

"Was your mother mad when she knew you'd found the papers?" she asked Karen.

"She's not my mother. 'Course she was mad. I don't have to listen to anything she tells me from now on. I don't even have to be home when she tells me to."

Jenny put the flattened silver paper in her pocket, where she found the dog key chains; she brought one out.

"Want one of these?"

"Where'd you get that?"

"Take it. I have lots more. I stole them."

"You stole them?"

"Sure. From the five and ten."

"My father'd beat me for that."

"I don't tell my mother, she'd beat me too."

"What if you get caught? You'll go to jail."

"They won't catch me. Anyway it's a big store. I wouldn't steal from a little store. But the big stores cheat us anyway."

"Says who?"

"Jamie told me. He told me about big business and stores and how they—" The word exploit floated in her mind, but she wasn't sure it was correct. She paused to remember Jamie's anger. "They don't pay the clerks enough, and they make everything cost too much, for poor people."

"Well I think you're pretty stupid to do it anyway."

"I think I'm pretty smart."

Was she even with Karen? Uneasily she felt the rifts. They were not alike, and she had put them further apart with her secret. Wanting to feel superior she also felt distance.

"Want to go to a movie in the Square?" Karen asked.

"No."

Karen got up. "Okay. Suits me. Who wants to go to the movies with a thief anyway?"

Karen walked away under the trees humming. Leaving Jenny with the key chain in her lap. Finally Jenny stood up stiff with cold and walked toward Charles Street. Dimly she wanted to go home to get warm. Ice rimmed the edge of the pond; on the island ducks sat in their blown-up feathers. It would be warm at home. It wasn't any good to walk by herself; Karen had left her abruptly and with nothing to look forward to. A day that held out something and vanished on her. No place in the world to go. If she went home Jamie would be practicing the piano, which he was good at while she wasn't. He would be hunched forward, frowning, and soft with the keys, and she was not allowed to interrupt. And her mother would tell her she looked like a mess and what had she and her fellow traveler been up to? Jenny rummaged around in her head to find someone she liked. But came up only with the soldier, and she had not managed to get him.

Jenny stood at the edge of the Public Gardens and looked back. The globes on the bridge flickered on, throwing spikes of light down into the water. Everyone looked very old, huddled in the cold, and watching their feet because of the lumps of ice on the walks. Jenny was beginning to shiver; her rib cage and shoulders heaved under her old coat, and she held her jaws firmly together until the shivers extended to her arms and hands; she locked them over her stomach and wondered where Karen was. Somewhere on the subway, rocking off to Cambridge by herself, with no need to go home again ever. Jenny's mother called Karen a fellow traveler because Karen's father, a diemaker in Cambridge, was a Communist. Jamie had more to say to Karen than to Jenny; they talked about Joe McCarthy, and once he laughed with his head back for a long time because Karen said: "Don't tell anyone my father's a Communist or McCarthy will get him." Jenny was never able to make Jamie laugh; if she said anything that took more than one sentence he looked at her out of his spotted green and yellow eyes below their parched lids, a faintly mocking, faintly gentle glance, the kind of look she delivered her own face in the mirror. But mostly Jamie lectured her, and then pushed her hair back out of her eyes and left the room. And she had never done anything for Jamie. She could not steal anything grown-up enough for him, and in any case whatever she stole she locked up in her chest at home and never looked at it again. Only the times she stole candy, she shut herself up in her room and ate it all, stuffed it all down, and later threw up, her knuckles white and bony on the toilet seat, kneeling and throwing up and crying until her mother came in and told her that since she hadn't eaten anything bad all day, and supper had only been lamb chops and peas, it must be Jenny's nerves that made her sick. And she made nerves sound like a filthy disease, so that Jenny dragged herself into bed without caring whether her mother came in to see how she was or not.

Jenny stared along the Gardens, at the lumpy figures of people, with no one small enough to be Karen. She thought of the subway rocketing along, the dark tunnels, the stations blurring out of the dark, and then the dismal clutter of Harvard Square and Karen scuffling along. Jenny was shivering so badly that she leaned against the fence; her spine vibrated between the railings. Once she had bought Jamie a present. It was another season, while she and Karen were still sidekicks, and used to stroll in their blue jeans along Atlantic Avenue, near the docks. They talked in gibberish and gesticulated as they'd seen Italian shopkeepers do, describing circles with their hands, bringing various fingers together in mysterious coalition; pretending that they were refugees just off a ship, hands in pockets between conversations, kicking out their feet in old sneakers. One day a sailor tried to sell them a brown cigarette. "Here's a joy, girlies," he said, holding the cigarette just outside the slit of his pocket and smiling at them, she remembered, with pained eyes and a slashed mouth. Karen ran away; Jenny held the smile a second longer, and ran after her. "What *was* that, Karen?" "It was dope." They panted and held each other's arms. "Come on," Jenny said, and they laughed and ran after the sailor. For $2.00 he sold them the cigarette, the same slashed smile open on his teeth, and his eyes like two dull pennies without shine. His lips looked sore. The girls ran off. "I'm taking it home to Jamie," Jenny said. It was the first thing she had ever bought for him; her mother picked out his birthday and Christmas presents and claimed they were from Jenny as she did not trust Jenny's taste. But it wasn't a good choice of present, the brown cigarette. One evening when she and Jamie were alone in the apartment he lit it. He kept a pack of stale Camels in his bookcase behind the books and could draw without coughing. Jenny watched him with the brown cigarette; he smoked and looked watchfully into corners. A long silent time passed. Then he stood up, swayed on his feet, and his eyes came to Jenny. "What are you looking at me for?" he cried. "Goddam you, girl, quit looking. You don't have to look. You're my twin. You're my twin sister." Jenny saw the bones in his face and felt her own bones straining under the skin; she sat as though whipped. In front of her Jamie stood swaying and talking: "It makes me sick to see you. You're just like me. It's like looking in the mirror when you feel ugly and sleepy, and that's *you*." He put the brown stub in her fingers and she took three or four choking puffs until the room spun, then she went to bed and cried, his face against her closed eyelids swollen stupid and ugly, shifting into her own face with its pale hair and swollen cheeks, the white pinched lips of herself throwing up. She found herself in the bathroom with the taste of vomit in her mouth. Calling, she ran out for Jamie and found him dozing on the sofa in the living room. He smoothed back her hair and laughed at her, called her a dope fiend, and they went into the kitchen where between them they drank a quart of milk. That was last summer, but she still felt odd with Jamie; sometimes he smiled and called her his twin, though he was two years older. He was very good at friendship and no good at sense.

It was evening. The street lights stood out behind Jenny's shoulders. Karen must be somewhere by now, somewhere warm. In the movie house, or Brigham's eating a hot fudge sundae. Jenny's ankles were clamped together and she hugged herself, trembling, against the fence. She could feel her ankle bones against each other, and feel the piercing hip bones under her clamped arms. Someday she would be old like the figures picking their way along the ice; old and slow and wearing a thick coat, with someplace to go. Well she had someplace to go: there was a big drugstore where she occasionally stole candy, though it was risky; they had mirrors. She pushed herself forward from the fence and walked fast, with stiff cold legs and feet.

Inside the drugstore Jenny hung around aimlessly with an eye on the candy rack. She found herself examining bathing caps in plastic bags. Flushing, she jerked away: no one needs bathing caps in winter, they would know she was stalling. She stiffened and did not know what to do next. Everyone must be watching. She approached the candy counter with nervous eyes; she felt them in spite of themselves looking too cautiously at people. She went hot inside her coat, inside her skin, and yet she was still shivering. It wasn't working. The man at the cash register had spotted her, was watching her awkwardness. She was just a kid who stole, like any other, and needed watching. Almost she begged him to let her get away with it, to look the other way; there was nothing else left to her day. Her mouth opened and she heard herself say with insistent shyness: "What time is it, please?" He looked at her and looked at his watch, briefly, with a flick of eyes that zoomed back to her. "It's five after five," he said. "Thank you very much," Jenny said, and left the store, hurrying, to prove her innocence.

It was dark. Jenny stood outside the drugstore trying to know where to go. If she could think long enough she would find a place. A woman in a coat without buttons stood shuffling her feet, peering across the concrete at Jenny. They shared the sidewalk, neither one moving. The girl looked at those feet and saw them wrapped in cloth through which two heavy brown shoes poked; there was a gap between the sole and the shoe. Moving her eyes up she saw a hem loose below the coat, as though a dog had torn at it. They shared the strip of pavement, examining each other. Jenny suddenly felt what she looked like, as though nobody had looked at her all day. A thin child in a brown coat, with averted eyes, a child sprung out on the streets and ill at ease, with a nervous cramping mouth. It was not what she had thought she was, but she felt it jarringly, as though she had seen herself reflected in a window. And suddenly the woman's face was close to her own: a pink and gray face with receded eyes, a porous nose, and a mouth slack and quivering, her pale-pink crusted lips stirring, not from cold but from some nervous inner action. She smelt, like the tunnels leading to subways, a familiar rank smell. Jenny fixed her eyes on that mouth and stepped back; but the woman stepped with her.

"Little girl," she said, and Jenny raised her eyes to meet the woman's; they were crossed with red lines and mushy at the edges as though dissolved into the skin; like sour milk at the edges.

"Little girl, do you see that white stuff, do you see it? Do you know what that is?" She grabbed Jenny's arm and pointed at the sidewalk. Something streaked the cement with white, but the girl went blank. She stood riveted on her feet. "Do you know what that white stuff is? Little girl, do you know what it is?"

Jenny shook her head and a fascinated voice stuck in her throat.

"Do you see that white stuff? Do you see it little girl? Do you know what it is? I'll tell you. I'll tell you what it is." Her eyes came closer, till they were out of focus, two murky blobs cut across with red. "I'll tell you what it is, little girl. You never saw such white stuff, did you?"

Jenny felt the hand on her elbow, not a grasp but an urgent resting. Her murky eyes blotted out Jenny's vision; only a blur spreading out from fat; age, the fat that kept her from shivering as Jenny was shivering. Their eyes held.

"Do you know what that white stuff is, little girl? I'll tell you what it is. That's pigeon shit." And she let go of Jenny's arm.

Jenny bolted. She collided with a dead wall and righted herself, her eyes swinging over the street, the end of the Pepper Pot Bridge, the raised subway stop like a fortress over their heads. Her eyes swung forward, loaded with tears and spilling them as she stood. The drugstore threw a little chilly light onto the street where the woman stood, contemplating the sidewalk. Jenny held herself forward from the wall with one hand; cold air matted her throat. She propelled herself forward into the light, and stood shivering in front of the woman. Her legs were collapsing under her, but with an effort she held herself in place.

"Good night," she whispered. "Why don't you go home?"

"Home. Yes. The world is loaded with pigeon shit. Shit all over." She dragged her eyes up to Jenny's level, eyes crossed with veins like a road map leading nowhere. "They threw my husband out. They threw him in. 'Cause he's black and red, and he's golden, girl, he's golden, to me he's golden. May the shit fall on Washington, may the shit fall on their heads, on their capitalist heads!" She leaned forward at Jenny, who stood her ground, shivering and weeping. "They grow white from the shit, they turn gray in Washington from the shit, girl." Then her hands moved, swept, rose, and the woman's face lifted, raising its soft swollen lines to the drugstore light. "Oh no, I got nothing against the pigeons. Innocent creatures like yourself. May they flap their wings forever."

Jenny swayed but stood. Her eyes threw out tears in squirts. She wanted to reach and touch the woman, but her hands clasped over her ribs as though to keep her body from flying apart; she was shivering so much she thought her bones would unhinge. In the dim light the woman turned her head up toward invisible pigeons.

"Figuratively speaking, it's pigeon shit." And she produced a smile. "Figurative, I call it. Figurative shit. But child you're quaking. Don't you ever come here again, child, it was here they turned him in, they run drugs here, child, and they snatched him, my golden husband. Those white-shitted cops forgot him for years when he was just black. Now they see him 'cause he's red, my man's red, and if you're red nowadays, if you're red they shit on you. Just 'cause he's black and he's red. My golden man is in . . ." She stepped into the darkness, leaned against the wall, and contemplated Jenny. "You're shivering child. So golden and so shivering!"

Jenny's hands in her pockets encountered the last of the silver-wrapped chocolates. "Do you like chocolate?"

"Do I? Do I like chocolate? When he came home to me evenings, he brought me . . ." Her voice dropped and huddled: ". . . oh every kind of . . . chocolate."

Jenny reached out a handful of the candies. The woman pocketed them and crouched against the wall, swaying and stumbling to steady herself there. Jenny put out her hands for her, and cried out loud. A policeman emerged from the drugstore, shook out his cuffs, and winked into space. Smiling, he brushed Jenny aside, his hands powerful on the woman's sluggish body.

"Well, Mrs. Hull, hello there. Go home now little girl," he said with a deft smile.

"Good night," Jenny whispered to the woman.

"Good night child," broke the old voice.

Jenny stood on the corner and watched the figures staggering, the blue cop and the crumpled woman. And the sidewalk, because of the old buildings and the subway protrusions, was white in the street light, streaked white. It was, very simply, pigeon shit.

Jenny turned corners running. Heading straight for home. The same streets she covered coming home from school. She passed houses familiar through tears. But most familiar was a blankness of mind that accompanied those tears. Her mind was blank as she ran up streets. She had no idea how she had spent the afternoon or why it was dark. It was very dark. Though she knew every corner to turn, she could not remember their street names; each corner blurred past and she was uncertain if she would recognize the next one; until she encountered it, it too was familiar but nameless, and blurred by. With no particular desire to go home, she ran for it as though pursued; there she would be sheltered from herself. And though she knew she would reach home by this blind run and search for nameless street corners, she could not even think what home looked like; she only knew that when she saw it, it would appear to be home. Clues bloomed up in the darkness.

At the street door of their building Jenny pulled out her

keys on a flat, silver Swedish key chain her mother had given her. With a start she remembered her mother, and the silver key chain, and many things. She unlocked the door and went in. All the way up the stairs to their apartment her hands met up with onslaughting clues: the round banister knob at the turn of stairs, the receded niche on each landing, one supporting an enormous Chinese jug with a notched tile base, another protecting the statue of a girl whose cool white feet resisted the pressure of Jenny's fingers. She unlocked their apartment door. In the living room Jamie was sitting sideways on the piano stool, one of his Camels in his hand, bunched up and staring at the floor.

"Jamie," she whispered. He didn't like to be called Jamie any more. "Jim," she whispered.

He looked up, flicked his ashes on the rug, and rubbed them in with his foot.

"Hi Jen."

"Where's Mother?"

"She went to some cocktail party. She'll be home for supper."

"Jim, she'll smell the smoke."

"I'll open the window. So—hello Beauty."

"Hello Beast." Jenny flushed. Though she was still shivering, her face went hot. She felt sweat under her arms and along her ribs. Trembling and flushed she faced him across the rug. His eyes swept hers, left, and caught.

"What's up Jenny? D'you see a bad movie? You look wild . . ." And he smiled, his tentative questioning smile. "Take off your coat, Jen, your face is getting red." Jenny dropped her coat and fell into a chair.

"Jim, why'd you laugh when Karen said that about her father and Joe McCarthy?"

"McCarthy and his crew aren't interested in a die-maker in Cambridge. Why, has she been bragging about him?"

"She doesn't brag. She didn't say anything about him. But I met a woman and I don't think her husband was any bigger than Karen's father but they put him in jail because he's a Communist." And she told Jamie about the woman and her Negro husband, without mentioning the pigeon shit. Jamie sat forward on the piano stool with his knuckles together.

"It sounds like he just got caught for selling dope, Jen."

His voice was low, because Jenny was crying again, holding her coat over her ankles and licking under her wet nose. "No," she said. "She said the cops always knew about that, but only threw him in jail when they found out he was a Communist."

"Look Jen, you better stay away from crazy old women and sailors with cigarettes. You get in trouble and you get shook. Look at you Jenny! What are you bawling for?" Jamie got up and threw his Camel in the fireplace, arched his back, and opened the window to let out the smoke. "Take it easy. Okay?" And he pushed her hair back, over her ears, and gave her a handkerchief. She blew her nose and knuckled the tears off her cheeks, watching Jamie walk out of the room. And a little pain rose, familiar and total: she remembered the soldier stepping out with his gun resting over his shoulder, his beaked nose. She wished she had not thrown away the soldier who lay on his belly. Any soldier was better than none.

A long time later her mother swept in, smelling good, and sparkling with jewelry and darkened eyes.

"Jenny, what have you been into? You're a sight."

"Sorry, Mother."

"Go wash up before we eat."

"I'm not hungry," said Jenny. She gripped her knees.

"No of course not. I suppose you and Karen ate ice cream all afternoon."

Jenny stirred. "I'm just not hungry." She remembered Karen walking away by herself under the trees, humming.

"Jenny, will you hang up your coat and go wash your face." Her voice was a level anger. She stood, smelling of perfume, holding her good coat neatly over her arms, in a black dress with sparkling buttons. She looked pretty, and agitated with the excitement of her party, focusing on Jenny with her anger, because she had come home to find Jenny a sight. Jenny got up. She had stopped shivering. Hunching herself small, she went to her room, past Jamie's door with its crack of light.

She wished she could ask him to come in. He was nice when he said, What are you bawling for? or something like that. He said it with a low teasing voice, a little tough, and then pushed her hair back or knocked on the top of her head and said, Solid mahogany. It was Benny who had first knocked on her head like that. So that she wished Jamie and his friends would all come into her room; Benny and Goldberg especially; they always called him Goldberg. Goldberg was shy, with nervous eyes that laughed easily, almost tenderly, and Benny was lanky and comical; he had curly yellow hair like a baby angel. But Goldberg was the best. Goldberg was one of the best she had ever known.

Her mother liked Jamie's friends. She said they were intellectual and serious boys, just as Jamie was serious, particularly about the piano. Not like her and Karen. Once her mother said she and Karen looked like slum kittens. It was meant to hurt, but it didn't, especially.

Jenny sat on her bed and put her bare feet up under the quilt. She didn't unfold the quilt because then she'd have to fold it up again; her mother was very fussy about things like that. Maybe after supper Jamie would come in himself. She wondered where Karen was, and if she was shivering too on the dark streets. It was always icier in Cambridge.

She heard her mother call and went to the door. She'd try to eat. But her mother wasn't calling her for supper. "Jenny, the phone."

Jenny ran into the living room.

"Karen!"

"Jen, I'm in a phone booth, right near you. I can't go home. Can I come over? Will your mother mind?"

"Just come. Are you okay, Karen?"

"Yeah sure. See you, Jen. Thanks."

"Where have you been?" Jenny asked, but Karen had hung up.

The lights were on all over the apartment and she could smell supper and hear her mother in the kitchen; it smelled like stew, last night's stew being heated up. Her mother's dressy shoes stood by the sofa, and there was a glass of whiskey with ice crowded up to the top. She would like to earn one smile from her mother; she was pretty when she smiled, soft, and a little sad; her smile was weary and appreciative. To earn that smile Jenny went into the bathroom and washed her face, washed it hard in hot water, letting the hot water run over her wrists. She was beginning to warm up. Goldberg had told her how to run hot water over your wrists when you're cold, and cold water when you're hot. It had been a long time since she'd been hot, since last summer. The last hot day in September she played catch with Goldberg on the Common, while

Benny and Jamie sat on a bench and smoked. She guessed Jamie smoked about four cigarettes a day; not enough to stunt his growth, he said. She wouldn't know; he looked pretty small anyway, not as tall as Benny. Goldberg told her she had a good throw, that she threw like a boy. They arched the ball high at each other, long slow spins up into the sky. When they got tired they walked down to a water fountain and ran cold water over their wrists. Goldberg flicked a little water on her forehead. Not the way Benny would have done it, kiddingly and playing. Goldberg stroked the drops of water along her sweaty forehead and handed her his tender smile with the flecks of amusement in his eyes. Jenny and Goldberg walked back to the bench; their shoes were dusty, and summer was withering up in the browned leaves and yellowed grass. Goldberg sat down and took one of Jamie's Camels, and Jenny stood, shifting her weight and laughing because there wasn't any room for her on the bench; the three boys were spread out. They kept looking at her and smiling, and Benny kept saying: "What are you standing up for?" Finally they squeezed up to let her sit, they pulled her onto the bench between Goldberg and Jamie, and both Goldberg and Jamie put their hands across her shoulders. She was very pleased and went right on smiling.

Jenny was in the bathroom when Karen rang the bell. Quickly she grabbed a towel to dry her face and arms, and dropped it at the doorway as she ran to the hall. But her mother was already at the hall door, and Jenny could hear Karen's voice from about half a flight down, and not coming any closer.

"I called Jenny, Mrs. Wolf. She said it was okay."

"Don't you think you've been hanging around enough

for one day? God knows what you girls were up to, but Jenny is filthy and exhausted. I'm sending her to bed early and I think you should just go home, Karen. This minute." Her voice was very even and very angry.

Jenny tried uselessly to get past her mother at the door. She couldn't see Karen standing on the stairs.

"Jenny, you girls have no right trailing around after dark, worrying your parents to death. Now go get Jamie for supper. I'm sending Karen home."

"You weren't worrying to death about me, you were at a party."

"I was speaking of Karen's mother. She must be frantic. Just go on home, Karen. I'll call your mother."

"She can't go home," cried Jenny. "She doesn't have a mother."

"Shut up damn you, I told you not to tell," came Karen's disembodied voice.

"You girls are so charming to each other it's no wonder you can't stay apart."

"Let her come in, let her stay, Mother, please. Let her in."

"Go home, Karen. I don't want you girls to get in the habit of wandering around at night and showing up in houses where you weren't invited. If you wanted to come for the night you should have asked me, and brought your things along. Now go home, Karen. I'll call your mother and tell her you're coming." She shut the door.

"You can't!" cried Jenny. "It's cold out."

"She should have gone home earlier. Call Jamie for supper, Jenny, and stop crying."

Jenny opened the door and called down the stairs.

On the second floor Karen's face leaned out to look up

the stairwell. The bulb was harsh on her face, which was pinched and white and swollen like a peeled hard-boiled egg.

"I'm sorry, Karen."

"Sure. You can't help it. I'll see you at school."

Her face withdrew and Jenny listened to her steps and then the downstairs door shutting.

Please please God please. Jenny thought she was warm, but as she walked down the hall to Jamie's door she began to shiver again, through her ribs. Knocking, she went into his room with a plunge.

"Jim?—What are you doing?"

Jamie had a map spread over his knees.

"Looking at the New York subway map. I want to figure it out before we get there. I don't want to act like a jerk, asking people the way all the time. Here, take a look."

"Are we really going to move there?"

"Of course. What did you think it was, a joke? On June 30 we hit the big town." He smiled, pleased with himself; it must be a line from one of his favorite mystery books.

"Won't you miss—miss your friends? Benny, Goldberg?"

"Yeah, I'll miss them. They can come visit on vacations. Look Jen, here's where we'll live, West Tenth Street. There are two subways nearby, on Sixth Avenue and Seventh Avenue. See?" He traced it out, the unknown streets, the subway lines. Jenny rode the MTA every day to school in Cambridge. She looked at the lines on the New York map and felt bad. She got her change for the subway from the same man every morning; he was a hunchback with a big balding head and soft eyes. Once he asked her

her name, and after that called her Jenny every morning. "Good morning, Jenny." Sometimes he got it wrong and said, Good morning, Jeanie. Even when she didn't need change she got it from him. He was a nice man.

"I'll miss Karen."

"She can come for vacation too."

"Mother doesn't like her." Jenny pushed the map away. She might as well go to New York as anywhere.

"How come you're still shivering?"

"I don't know."

Knees gripped together, she was sitting on his bed. The total afternoon came back; she saw the hunched figures, the iced walks in the Public Gardens, felt the fence railing against her spine, saw the sky go white and frozen and then darken from the top downward, saw the woman's blurred eyes and heard the pitch of her voice. She stared into Jamie's room to make it take shape again and be substantial.

"What was all that fighting about in the hall?"

"Mother wouldn't let Karen in. She sent her home."

"Where has she been all this time?"

"Karen? I don't know. She doesn't want to go home. Mother made her."

Jamie's voice jerked, in his own kind of anger. "She should have—given her money for a—taxi, at least. It's pretty late. She treats Karen like—shit."

Jenny laughed. Shit was the word. "Like pigeon shit," she laughed.

Jamie laughed. "Don't swear, girl. Girls shouldn't swear till they're eighteen." But he went on laughing.

"She treats me like shit too," said Jenny, doubled up with laughing, and choking all the time, grabbing for breath.

"Hey, what's gotten into you tonight, Jen? Jenny, quit it. Stop laughing, Jenny—Jenny! Cut it out. What's the matter with you?"

Jenny dropped her head down between her knees, laughing and coughing till she drooled on the rug. "Talk some more, Jamie."

"Jim," he corrected, out of his own testiness.

"Jim."

"What's wrong with you, Jenny? Was Mother mean to you?"

"No. It's all mixed up, Jamie. Jim."

"Look, let's go eat, or Mother'll be hopping. You okay?"

She had knocked off laughing abruptly, and nodded, her eyes clamped onto his face.

From under his parched lids his spotted eyes obscurely took her in, then lidded themselves. "Let's go. If you feel bad kick me under the table."

Jamie folded up the map neatly; he always did everything carefully. He ran his fingers up through his hair so that it stood up straight and short and spiky.

"Can I use your brush?" she asked.

"Sure."

Her face in the mirror was reddened and her eyes puffed. She brushed her hair until the tangles were gone and it fell to her collarbone in two neat flat lines like a big helmet. Then she wiped off the tear smudges with spit, and made sure all the buttons of her sweater were buttoned in order. In the mirror she saw Jamie at the door tucking in his shirt, hitching up his pants, though they slid down again on his thin hips. So they went to supper.

Jenny sat down in front of her plate. She wasn't going to forgive her mother for driving Karen out. But her ribs quivered, her arms felt hot and light. She wondered where the cop had taken the woman. She wondered where Karen was; she might walk all night. And she thought of Karen's father, his cracked mouth below the pink-rimmed glasses touching her forehead like a priest. He spat out the tobacco onto his fingertips and put the cigarette back in his mouth. He took off his glasses often, revealing bruised eyes and soft pouches of skin under those eyes, little soft gray pouches of sickliness. Sometimes at supper in her own house she shut her eyes and pretended he was sitting at the other end of the table. Tonight she shut her eyes and placed the soldier there; he sat easily, with his arms on the table and his fingers relaxed. The little pain came up in her throat; she missed him. But then he said, Hello, Jenny Marx. His face shifted, aged, he wore pink-rimmed glasses, he leaned across the table and kissed her forehead.

Jenny opened her eyes.

"The stew's good," she said, fastening her look on her mother. "I feel better. I was so cold before."

So her mother smiled at her, with her tired grateful smile. It was worth a lot to receive that smile. Jenny would rather be loved than known.

Sky in Winter

The light had gone down behind buildings, the sky was dull dull, white at the edges with cold. The sky like an obscure hand over the earth. Hand over hand, indefinitely hands over the earth. In their grip. In the grip of the sky. The white evening of December had shut down upon the city and a still air distributed itself among the streets. The streets bundled people along; their movement and the bright scarves came and went under the small moons of light and muffled up a stir of Christmas vibration. Among the evening shoppers Stan walked on a fixed line, like a man on an urgent errand. The cones of light glanced down on his raised stubborn face; in the darkness between them he looked up at the blur of city lights around the rim of the sky, a blur that ascended, fading, into the darkening space.

He came across Broadway toward a large store window which set a contained block of light on the sidewalk and shone yellow and warm in the dusk. Through that window he could see a corner of the desk with the cash register, the end of the bookshelves, and by the glass door two young men huddling into their coats and talking to someone he could not yet see. It might be Allie; but it might be Jessie herself. He stood on the island in the mid-

dle of the street while cars flashed by, looking beyond
them with impatience at the young men talking over their
shoulders into the hidden space of the bookstore; underneath, the subway pounded into the station sending hot
air up through the grate and under his coat. Then the
traffic stopped and he cut diagonally across the street, intent on seeing if the person from whom these young men
could not tear themselves away was, as he supposed, Jessie. To his surprise it was another customer, a lean boy in
a trench coat, and Stan pushed open the door with a
hint of urgency. For now he saw the whole length of the
narrow store and Jessie was not there. Allie, behind the
register, leaning on her elbows and eating a cookie, sat
back on the stool and wiped her hand across her mouth
like a child.

"Hello Stan. Jessie's downstairs. She'll be right up. Or
shall I call her?"

"Yes, will you?"

Stan walked back between the stacks, his eyes running
over the signs on the shelves: Astronomy—he paused, but
he knew all the titles—Biology, Chemistry. At the far end
against the wall he would come to Russian Novels, and
slowly but directedly he made for them. He was intent on
arriving at the furthest corner where, among the Russian novels, Jessie would find him. There was something
about being found among the Russians.

"Hello Stan," said a voice from the Psychology books as
Stan walked by. Harris, a graduate student in Stan's de-
partment, straightened up with three books in his arms.

"Hello," said Stan, passing on. Getting to Jessie was like
running a gauntlet. Psychology books for an astronomer?
But perhaps Harris needed them. Stan would not stop to
talk. But Harris padded after him.

"I didn't see you at the seminar today."

"No. I didn't go."

"You should have. It helps to be seen."

Stan turned to face this small earnest man, his eyes flat on Stan's face. And from those eyes Stan saw again that he himself was the best student, a kind of genius they said, and that it was also said that he snubbed the other graduate students. He did not know the eagerness Harris felt, the need just to be seen as interested. If Stan never set foot in the University the professors would not care, whereas Harris showed up everywhere, his eyes earnest, his briefcase yawning with notes. Now again Stan had snubbed someone, pressing on to that furthest corner where Jessie would find him.

"Where's Jess? She was up here a minute ago. That funny chap—you know—Petterson, who's in Chaucer— tubby fellow—was entertaining us with some of the tales Chaucer *didn't* write."

"Jessie's downstairs," Stan answered, and was suddenly standing humbly in front of Harris. Why did all the people who drifted in and out of the store call her Jess? How did they manage to stand around with Jessie laughing and telling stories? Even Harris, with his earnestness and adopted Englishisms, simply dropped by to have a laugh. While Stan himself came along to drag her away from all that; for fit as he was for some things, he was not fit for standing around laughing with her at fat Petterson's tales. He was envious: therefore angry.

"No one calls her Jess except her mother and kid sister," he said, out of his humility and anger.

"Sorry about that. I'll be seeing you." With a dip of his head Harris turned and carried his books to the desk.

Stan stood under the bright light, his collar turned up behind his black hair. His overcoat fell straight to his knees, stiff and covering him like a soldier's coat. He was a straight nervous young man, his pale skin flushing with cold up to his temples. He was flushed now with cold and distress. The thick rims of his glasses and the shining lenses hid the hurt eyes, giving him a studied look, for he continually moved his head so that the glasses flashed, glinting blindly on his face. He had cheeks flat as a chisel from cheek bone to chin, and a soft humorous mouth. But even when he laughed the glasses flashed like two round warnings. Standing between the stacks he put his hands carefully into his coat pockets and faced forward like a sentinel.

The door opened and Jessie came in. A little following gust of wind pushed her light hair over her cheeks and she glanced around easily, brushing back her hair with a small hand and smiling indiscriminately until she spotted Stan. He saw her pale joyous eyes, her triangle face with the serious little nose. Every day she worked in front of that glass wall so that all Broadway saw her round small neck and the slope of her shoulders; but he had married her and marked her as his with a gold ring. Nonetheless it bothered him that she smiled so vaguely so easily before he came into focus. He let her walk right up to him before he indifferently took out one hand from his pocket and put it up to his face where it adjusted the glasses. Then she was kissing him and pulling him to the desk.

"So you're off," said Allie. "Your first vacation in two months!"

"Well I need it," Jessie laughed. She was wearing a blue smock over her dress and she took it off and hung it neatly on a hook. "Take care of all that money and my smock and I'll see you."

"Sure. Ciao," said Allie with brief affection in her eyes.

Outside Jessie said, "Some vacation, staying home all day or going out to buy toothpaste."

"You can sleep."

The cold air fortified him. They would go home. It did not even bother him that she had accused him of not being able to take her away and give her a proper vacation. Since they had been married she had only had a few days off from work, and in the evenings she proofread for a publisher. I *could* get a good job, she sometimes said plaintively, but it's nice to work near home. Anyway I have no ambition. Tell me about the stars.

They turned down a dark side street away from the Christmas shoppers and then she was a mystery to him again. Not the girl he had first seen sitting erectly on a stool by the large glass store front; he had walked by just to see her round strong arms resting on the desk. That was spring, and now he had married her, but still she sat and he had an uneasy notion that she, Jessie, was a creature in a glass bowl, was encased behind glass, that she sat like a figure in a child's glass bowl so that should he get his hand around it and shake it, snow flakes would swarm around her. But she would sit even so with her bare round arms and her easy smiling face. If he could shake the whole thing up and make it snow cold inside she would sit with her smiling triangle face. Also when he got her home he could not get over the idea that she was set back in glass and even natural disasters could not disturb her.

So that in the dark, alone with him, away from Broadway, she gathered a small mystery about her. He felt a private lust for her.

"I'm not even going to read proof," she said in a small voice. "Can I just sleep?"

"You just sleep."

"Are you working tonight?"

"A little."

"Then we'll look at stars."

"It's getting cloudy."

"Then we'll multiply distances," she said cheerfully. "If light travels eleven million miles a minute . . ."

He was not sure: did she mock him with her curiosity about astronomy? She made models on the floor with oranges and apples of the universe and then set things in motion, kneeling above them, her hair falling over the little galaxy. "If this is the Milky Way and this is the sun . . ." Very seriously she moved the outer stars, two rotten apples and some walnuts. Was she in earnest? Or she set the fruit out as galaxies and spun each one, sent them out in space. Once she flung a handful of nuts on the floor and cried: "Is that it? How the universe is expanding?" Yes, he said. It was just like that.

"I wish you didn't have to go back to work at all," the astronomer said as they got near their apartment. It was dark, he could speak. Although in the light his pale face would have flushed, knowing he had not enough money to let her quit.

"Why? I like it there, I really do. There are plenty of people. I'd get bored at home. I mean, you're always working. I wouldn't get to see you, staying at home."

"In a few years," he said stiffly, "I'll be teaching, maybe only twice a week. We'll have a family." He moved his face restlessly and touched his glasses. He was the University's genius but he wanted a child.

"Not yet. I like seeing people."

"I just wish it wasn't there. Your job."

"Why?"

"Everybody can see you."

"Well everyone in your classes can see you."

"It's different. You're behind glass."

She fell quiet and he thought: I said it. How absurd it was. Here she was with her hand in his pocket against his hand. It was morbid, thinking she was glassed-in. She was warm and quiet and wanted to sleep. He turned his face happily, blindly in the dark.

In the apartment she switched on all the lights and fell into a chair.

"Oh I wish we were going away," she cried.

"Well we can't. In the summer we will. We'll go to Maine. You can rest this time."

"I don't want to rest. I'm not tired."

"But you said you wanted a week off."

"I do. But I want to *go* somewhere."

"Look Jess, we can't. We'll go somewhere Sunday."

"Where? The Cloisters?" she said sarcastically.

"We'll borrow a car. We'll go somewhere."

He left her sprawled in the chair and went into the bedroom to work.

It was close to midnight when the astronomer pushed everything back on the table and lit one more cigarette. Then he knew it had been very still in the living room since the phone rang a long time ago. The stillness struck him. He got up and opened the door confidently. Jessie was sitting with her chin on the windowsill, motionlessly sitting.

"Jess!" he said with more urgency than he had intended.

She turned her head, her cheek on her palm.

"What have you been doing, Jess? You could have gone to bed."

"I'm not sleepy."

He came and sat on the radiator; they looked out into the dark sky. "If the stars were out," he began, to remind her of her persistent curiosity which he often dismissed, "and Orion were right above us, what would we see?"

"The Horse's Head."

"How far away is it?"

"Oh—billions of miles," she said helplessly, and laughed.

"What have you been thinking about?"

"I really want to go away."

"Why, Jess?"

"I'm a wreck," she said casually and moved away from him. "But I know we can't."

"No, wait a minute. What do you mean?"

She was walking into the middle of the room; then she stood and looked at the wall. He saw her put her hand up to push back her hair and he saw the back of her neck briefly before the hair fell forward again. Irrelevantly he thought: I hope we have a daughter. Then she burst into tears and flung herself on the sofa.

It took a moment for his nerves to catch up with his eyes. Then he rushed toward her as though guilty.

"I'm so frightened," Jessie cried. "Please let's go away."

"Jessie! What is it?"

"I'm being threatened."

"Threatened? What do you mean?"

"Someone called up and threatened me. Tonight."

"But that's just a crank. They never do anything."

"No no, it's someone I know."

Stan sat up. Something uneasy moved in his brain. "Who do you know?"

"Nobody. Someone from a long time ago. He threatened me."

He. So that was it. He.

"Well don't be angry, Stan, please. Really, before I knew you. I'm scared."

"Who is this guy? What is this all about?"

She was crying in a nervous, jerky way. But he could not put out his hands.

"Jessie! Who is it?"

"I knew him before I met you and then when I met you I wouldn't see him any more. And he . . . he was angry. Oh he's nuts, Stan; he's crazy but he called up tonight and said things . . ."

"What kind of things?"

"Like I'll be sorry, I'll pay for it, I should move away from here because he lives nearby and doesn't want me around—things like that."

"You'll be sorry for what?"

"Because I wouldn't see him again. After you. He's been calling me for months, to see me."

She started a shaking crying again and he sat stiffly away from her with a mind lucidly seeing into this. This he. He felt a relieving arrogance toward this crazy he.

"Where does he call you?"

"Here. Or at work."

"Does anyone hear you talk to him, at work?"

"Allie."

Allie. Who always said, Hello Stan. He lifted his face impatiently. That was just jealousy, that Allie should know about an old lover. He had no need to be jealous. He tried again seeing into this he. And then he saw.

"Have you seen him, Jess?"

"No."

"Since when?"

"Oh Stan," she cried frantically under the mass of her hair. "He comes into the store, he walks by. He's always walking by. He sees me. He's a nut, he keeps after me."

Stan shook his head slowly as though denying but also as though to see. Yes. He. Walking by. Coming into the store. The huge glass window in which Jessie sat all day. And this *he* had broken the glass, for him there was nothing inaccessible about Jessie. He had humiliated Stan. And Jessie was frightened now. She crouched like some throttled animal. So he could extract what he wanted, for in fear she would talk. She needed him. And with a dull glimpse he knew she had never needed him before.

"When were you last alone with him?"

"Oh Stan," she wept and then she cried evenly while he waited. She would tell him now in her own time. Stan sat erect and clairvoyant as though he knew it anyway.

Finally with a small voice diminished with contriteness she told:

"I did see him once. Well, he kept coming by the store and calling me up, even after we were married. He wanted to see me but I told him I wouldn't. Then one day he said could he see me for just five minutes, so I thought—I really did—he was going to apologize for bothering me, so I left the store and went around the block with him. It was that night last week when you were at the observatory and I worked till midnight—remember —so I walked with him and when we got to that alley he suddenly pushed me into it and hit me hard, in the face, and then he went for me with his fists, but I yelled and someone opened a window and then I ran. I went back to the store, into the basement. And then tonight he called me and threatened me. That's all. Sometimes I think he could kill me." She twisted around and grabbed his hand. He let it stay slack in her clutch.

"Did you ever tease him?"

"No."

"I mean, did you ever say you would see him, aside from the time you walked with him?"

She was quiet, not even crying. Stan stared around the room. There were her shoes side by side near the window. He stared at them. They looked detached, floating. They were her shoes. Something in his mind separated itself and crumbled.

"Yes. Earlier. But I didn't see him. I changed my mind."

"Why did you say you would see him?"

"For the same reason—I thought he just wanted to apologize."

"Jess, he could have said that in the store, in front of Allie as she knew about the phone calls anyway. In front of the customers. You didn't have to see him alone, you know that. You had all the rights. You're married and if you didn't want to see him . . ."

And so with agonizing relief he settled on what he had been trying to see. The beating episode was only a week old, and it was during this week that she had said she wanted to take some time off from work. Before that she was happy working . . . before that, when this *he* used to walk by, come in, call. The finality of this realization broke everything open in his head: it was as though everything else she had said had seeped like water into ice, and now the structure broke open.

Suddenly, swiftly, she twisted herself up and twiningly catching him around the neck she kissed him on the mouth. He kissed her as violently. Pushing her down he dragged her skirt up to her hips crushingly, so that she could not move, her mouth forced slack under his mouth.

In the dark she slept, dressed, curled up, fallen asleep in the middle of tears on the sofa. Stan sat by the window; rain collected on the screen, joining the mesh together in streams. The sky was rained out; there was nothing to see to console him. The slow turning of the stars went on behind a shallow curtain of rain that fell on that most insignificant planet the earth, perhaps falling only on New York which, though it was all that he knew and made up his whole world, was only a wet city flung on the Hudson. A great toll had been taken of his arrogance. And she was no more when the glass was broken than he had ever expected her to be; she was exactly what he had seen. With his forehead against the cold windowpane he let his mind ride up above the shedding clouds; and all that space was warmly, intimately filled with apples and nuts, with round oranges smelling of their skins. She, who had asked him all those questions about the stars and could not remember figures, had taught him more than he had taught her. The world would fly away like a handful of nuts and rot like apples; in its own time all that he knew would be gone, the sun and the earth, and his numbers would not hold it together. He went back to her on the sofa and curled up against her where they slept in their clothes cramped for space with their arms and legs gripping. Perishable they slept while the rain fell and stopped and withdrew, leaving a winter day over the Hudson.

Every Girl Has a Mother Somewhere

Some people are failures, and some are successes, and some people are successful failures; I group myself with the last. A young man who saw it coming and let it come; a young man who makes nothing of himself but does so with some style. A small betrayal of small convictions for the promises of someone unknown but superior—oh yes I always believed she was superior— and the discovery of ultimate flaws. She pretended to be one of my kind.

I saw it coming and let it come and now it's over. I was living my way, down; pot, and two poems published and no more to go. And she was a chick like any other, only she was slightly different. She smelled good and she wouldn't smoke grass and finally I quit too; she drank tea instead of coffee, and she looked brown like she'd been in the sun. Maybe she had; I didn't know where she came from or what kind she was. You didn't know things like that where I lived; some of us were rich and some poorer, some of us grew up in the Bronx and some in Indiana. We breezed through, no strings, and she seemed that way too. She arrived in my life one breezy spring day, as so many things arrive in a promising wind when the mind is gulled. She had a little bag of summer clothes; right then I should have known that her offering was to be only one season short. I took her in because her first words were: Man, if you don't give me a place to sleep I'll tell the neighbors. Standing on a breezy spring street I had to laugh. My neighbors were leaning on various windowsills, their elbows sooty—Puerto Ricans, and fair-haired prep school boys trying out the new life—and they watched us laughing in the sun. So I took her in. I thought she was amusing, and one of my own. She wasn't what you'd call a hippie, she was too smart for that. She came from way back there, rooted, and she looked like nothing could touch her. Only I didn't know what the roots were. Her fresh brown skin made me want to get out, and we got out together only I knew something was behind it because she went to the post office for a registered letter and didn't tell me what it was. So we got out together—Mikey and I—and came here.

I told Mikey about me because I wasn't ashamed; it wasn't fake for me, I didn't have money in the bank from parents on Park Avenue. My father works in a factory on Long Island and my mother makes hats; when I was a kid I had threads on all my clothes from sitting close to my mother while she snipped. I had my first sex in a basement with a black girl who worked me over till she got me right. It hasn't changed much since: I pick women who are talented at it. I went to college on a scholarship, a very bright boy, but I drifted to where I ended up living, because I liked the company of losers. My father always told us we shouldn't try for success, it kills you. Meaning that if it comes your way accidentally, grab it. He says that because he's a failure but he must have hoped we'd make it. One of my brothers is a doctor and my father's proud of that though he doesn't like the way he got there. Me, I couldn't stand trying, killing myself just to feel crushed like my father so I ducked out altogether. Sometimes I think I've got his mouth on my face, I can feel it go cramped with failure. So I chose a way to live where these things didn't apply; no one around me was going any particular way, up or out, and they weren't going away either. But I went away. I went away with Mikey. That's what I mean about being a successful failure; you have to have a certain amount of style to be standing around on your block in a spring breeze when a lovely and rich girl comes along—to be unemployed and a pothead and have a new life placed at your dirty feet.

Yes, we lived on Mikey. She said she had all this money to blow, so let's blow it together. It worked out okay because those gifted girls had taught me one or two things and I shook Mikey up like she'd never been shook up before. She didn't seem to have had much loving and what there was must have been quiet. I went right to her head and I stayed there.

I'm a loser and I know it. In my father's (unspoken) sense too: I have no career and nowhere to start one. But in my sense as well. I gave up serious studying and read what everyone read where I lived: Kierkegaard and the Tibetan Book of the Dead, Hesse and the I Ching, Jung and astrology. Nothing that I wanted to read or that hung together in my head. Sometimes I remembered with pride learning to read Middle English in college, but they didn't read Chaucer where I lived so I sold the book. Mikey didn't have to know; she saw me sitting over my books by the window and it was all the same to her. She read my books because she'd come empty-handed, but I always had the feeling they weren't her style. I didn't apologize for my books because that would have been like pointing out they were there; this way maybe she wouldn't notice. But one day I walked to town to buy a copy of Wordsworth: I wanted to read those lines about "the round ocean, and the living air,/And the blue sky." The round ocean. We were living by the ocean and sometimes it looked round to me. When I read Mikey those lines she was very happy like she recognized them and knew what they meant. "Whose dwelling is the light of setting suns,/ And the round ocean . . ." We were very happy by that ocean.

We rented a little gray shingled house she said a friend of hers usually took every summer, up on a cliff above the beach, with nobody in sight. I'd never been in a place like that; it was still, only the sea along the shore, and on windy nights the wind in the scrub trees. Mikey called them scrub, like stunted. Nobody came to the door, and I felt like I'd slept for a year. My hands quit shaking and I threw away my cigarettes. Sometimes I sat outdoors on the sandy earth just to sit in the stillness. Big ants ran over my ankles, and overhead the sky was streaked with clouds like birds' tails; flecks of gulls floated out, and the sea heaved up sulky and blue. At first I sat thinking it was quiet, but one day I listened. Birds in the trees, each kind of leaf registering the wind in its own way, gulls making gull cries in the sky, the dim pound of water under the cliff, the receding muffle of ocean along the shore: layers of sound, and I floated between them like my ears were rungs and I was climbing up and down among the noises. Suddenly the tears stung my eyes. My father was right and why kill yourself. It was the first supreme moment of my life.

We ate well. Our town was this fancy little town looking old and quaint and kept to look like that, but also like a little New York, with pocket-sized versions of Fifth Avenue stores. Mikey cooked big meals with lots of potatoes for me, and we even had smoked oysters with drinks, and with the drinks we mixed nothing but Schweppes. We had fun in that town; we strolled in with our sandals and clean striped jerseys and looked like everyone else there, brown and vacationing and buying exclusive foods. I felt I looked like everyone else and where I used to live I felt that way too. The line is narrow between the hippies, the losers, and the rich on vacation. Sometimes I wonder who got the styles from whom.

Then Mikey popped into the post office now and again and came out with her little straw bag containing secrets. But she never looked distressed so I never asked. Maybe she had a sick mother who was getting better.

But one day she said she didn't have a mother. She was dead. And her father'd shacked up with a bitch. Only she put no more inflection into these facts than if her parents had been dogs. So I didn't believe her and didn't need to.

Mikey: taller than I am by an inch but I'm not tall, hips wide and just right, with lines around her eyes like she's strained all the time, and short black hair that swings like a bell. She doesn't say too much and she doesn't need to. A quiet voice is an excellent thing in a woman and always has been since Will said it. And when she laughs she puts back her head and I can see a little triangle of white where the sun never gets, under her chin.

Was Mikey married and collecting alimony? Sure she was married, but there's no money there. He was a truck driver who sang folk songs on the side, or else he was some newspaper editor who had so many ex-wives and children and illegitimate kids he couldn't send her a nickel; or else he was a nice college boy and they got annulled so she got her name back and no money. Either way it's a lie. Though I've no doubt she knew them all.

Did I write poems on the beach? Some. But the old style was wrong and there was nothing new to go on. Once Mikey said she'd published a story in a good magazine. But I didn't believe that either.

I discovered something about Mikey's preferences and lack of style the night she walked into town to buy cigarettes and came back late with a fat rich boy. He had a baby face on a pinhead, and a big paunch under his dirty polo shirt. I always notice the rich are dirtier than the poor. I was proud of my clean jersey Mikey had washed for me that morning, and sat around to let him see it. Not that he'd come to the just conclusion. His eyes stayed on select points of Mikey's anatomy. We drank a lot and no explanations and then he got up and said Ciao and took off. I said Adios like I didn't speak the language and Mikey said Bye succinctly. I didn't even mind that she'd brought that rich kid home nor did I ask why she was so long in getting home. It was one of my habits of failure. She came up to me and put her arms around me and kissed me on the mouth like I was the world's first fresh orange to suck. That was to make me ask no questions and I'm easily bought.

We made friends with a man we called the American on the beach. Mikey had a beautiful bikini that looked very expensive but I didn't ask about that either. We walked out on the beach in the early evenings when the American was fishing. Mikey had seen him during the day with his family and she told him his daughter was beautiful; he was pleased by that and said she played the piano;

all his children were grand but that one was special. After that we were friends. He stood there in his trunks wearing an open blue parka, a square plaid basket by his feet, and with a very shiny fishing rod between his legs. Mikey said later it was obscene and I said she was. He was a regular guy. He knew the price of everyone's house along the shore and tried to look disinterested when we told him where we lived but like he saw something about us we didn't see—or maybe Mikey did; we had been classed. He had something to do with Wall Street or bankers and he only came out from New York on weekends to fish, while his family stayed all summer. It was good for him to get away from the city, you could see that and he said so. We stood on either side of him in the dusk and our voices faded out in the wind. You start to talk loud when you first get to the country and then you talk soft. We talked so softly in the gathering dark that only that rod with its shiny slender line held us in one place; our words whisked off like they didn't come from our own mouths and who knows who said them—they were gone down the beach. Sometimes the American landed a sand shark and let him thrash himself dead on the sand, and once a sting ray which he flipped over on his back and let him die too, panting and quivering his wings. It got so dark we could hardly see each other except that there was a strange luminous shine from the sea as though light came up from underneath and it made a dark moon figure of Mikey standing on the other side of the American. When we saw him on the beach during the day he was cool to us; his dreary wife was with him and a pack of kids eating chicken. Maybe his wife had charged him too often with watching bikini-girls on the beach, and Mikey was no exception.

But at dusk we stood around like old friends to watch the mysteries come out of the deep. When he caught a fish he killed it swiftly and put it in his plaid bag. He was our only friend.

We had been there about six weeks when I got curious. I didn't mind the lies because a girl like Mikey who was too good for me had a right to hide her past. Maybe she thought I'd feel inferior, because you can be sure if she came from anywhee it was from high up, or maybe she thought I'd feel scorn for her as I haven't much use for the rich. We never talked about rich and poor because she knew where I belonged and how I hated the rich and would never get there, even if I wanted to, except on her back. Once she knew that, there was no point making conversation about it. But the post office, and now phone calls from a booth in town, were present events—and I was part of her present. When it occurred to me that way, I was curious. I had a privilege to know. So I rummaged around and in her bureau found an envelope. There was a handwritten note saying: "I'll be back next week, call me and don't worry" and then the carbon of a deposit slip for five hundred dollars. The envelope was post-marked London and dated one week back. So she had called, and presumably she hadn't worried. About what? I looked around some more and found only deposit slips, five hundred each. Putting them back in my best Sam Spade style under her clothes I suddenly was aware of the whiff from the drawer, soft sweaters and jerseys smelling of talcum powder and salt, and I burst into surprised tears. I was going to be a loser here too and I knew it and with a kind of horror I knew I was in love with her and always had been although I had always told myself that I was giving her the goods in return for the money. I cried and stuffed one of her jerseys against my face. Curiosity had killed this particular cat.

A few nights later a crowd showed up. They'd been there before, that was clear. They greeted Mikey with kisses and hugs and helped themselves to the liquor from where nobody could guess, in a cabinet under the sink. They'd come in cars and judging from their clothes they'd come straight from the city. "We just heard you were back this year. We want a weekend party like the old ones," they said, though Mikey didn't look as though she agreed. I was introduced around like the cat, and I can't for the life of me remember a name. Hardly a face. Women in shift dresses, Puccis at least, men in linen jackets and soft shoes, a handsome black middle-aged man with a cast in his eye, and one little girl in a mini skirt if I ever saw one and a big Garbo hat and with a lot of talk about "her" theater. I talked to her mostly, she was more my type. We drank a lot and sat on the floor and gradually they took off their jackets and their shoes but the little girl kept on her hat. It was charming and I sat near her. Mikey hadn't looked at me so where else should I sit?

Then there was a roar and a screech and the slam of a solid car door that fit well in its frame. And a big handsome man came in and looked around in a hostlike way to see if we were all comfortable. We all were except me. Everyone got up and shook his hand and clapped him on the back and asked him how his trip was and said he looked as good as ever. He looked good to me without the comparison. Then they said, So you got away from the old girl for a while, and he said, Yes. The little girl introduced me. John was his name, that one stuck. Because then he went up to Mikey who was nervously trying to pat him on the back like everyone else, only he singled her out and took her face in his hands and kissed her on the mouth, on the throat, on the eyelids. Then we all sat down again and drank some more and I asked him how London was and he said, Rather lovely, and then he asked Mikey how her mother was and she said, Just fine, and that she hadn't expected him till next week. He didn't explain. Later he got to his feet and walked around in the other rooms and I saw all the lights go on and heard him opening drawers. He came back into the room looking into my copy of *Pensées* very casually like he was on his way to the bathroom, and then he engaged a few people in an undertone offhand way but I took the delicate hint and got to my feet. He came across the room at me and I asked for my book and he asked me to get out.

A guy like me doesn't get out for nothing. So I hit him in the stomach and he hit me in the jaw and everyone joined in and pulled us apart. Mikey stood back with a cornered look in her eyes, and John tossed me an arrogant glance like a penny. "Now what's all this? I pay rent on this house and I ask who I want to my parties," John said very reasonably.

I looked at Mikey and she didn't look back. I knew she had more to lose than I did, so I got out. I wouldn't make her give up anything. It was my small gesture, the loser's small moment of superiority.

It was late and I had no place to go so I went down on the beach. I stood at the bottom of the cliff and saw the breakers come up from darkness and topple white at some indefinable point where the beach was: it looked so close I was afraid to walk forward and also far enough away to be on the horizon. When I got used to the dark I made my way toward the water and then I could see the lights in the house above me and see figures passing the open windows. It looked cheerful and sounded cheerful and if I hadn't just come from there I'd have thought it was a good place to be. I walked along the beach until I couldn't see or hear them any more and then I curled up against a dune and slept. I've slept on park benches and the whole evening was like any episode from my past, only the setting was different. But I ended up drunk and sleeping just the same.

And that Mikey wasn't like anything from my past, and was unlikely to show up in my future.

I saw Mikey after that. It was winter and she was coming out of a store and I was walking to my job at Time-Life. Anyone can learn to proofread and so can I. I asked Mikey to have coffee with me and we went into a coffee shop and sat in the back. She looked all ready for anything and I gave her the chance. Where was her father? He's dead and this time she means it. He left her plenty of money but by the time he died she had it in for any man on two legs so she put the money away and let the men foot the bill. Didn't she have a right to? I don't know, I don't know all the details. Only she looked small and pinched and her hair was all poufed up and not like a bell any more, it didn't swing on both sides of her cheeks. I knew that she wouldn't smell of salt now and that she had more friends than we had had with only the American. She probably knew lots of Americans, and always had. Her mother lived in Chicago and that's true too, and she really did publish one story only she supposed I didn't think she was smart enough to, and she'd never written one again. She had tried to find out where I was living so she could send me my books; I didn't tell her I was living with my parents to save money and . . . and because I felt like starting again and getting to know them. So I said, Keep the books, and suddenly her eyes filled with tears effortlessly; they must have been there all along. She didn't apologize and she didn't explain and she didn't need to. We went outside bundling into our coats and stood shy and awkward under a sky cloudless as ice. Everyone was walking by going somewhere and I had somewhere to go and so had she I suppose but we stood as though waiting for someone to catch onto and be pulled like a train in any direction at all. Mikey's nose was red and her eyes blurred. She squeezed up her shoulders and said Good-bye and fell in behind a woman with a shopping bag. I let myself be persuaded across the street by a kid with a delivery wagon and though it wasn't in the direction of the Time-Life Building I walked very fast.

Melissa Savage

Every other day Melissa Savage came into town for her mail; also her groceries of course, or some envelopes, soap, and once a short yellow lobsterman's slicker. But the mail was her real reason for coming, everyone knew that. In her brown felt hat with the dipping brim, her sky-blue turtle-neck sweater, her brown skirt that buttoned down the front and was missing the bottom button, and old sandals that crisscrossed over the thin bones of her feet, she stood in the line that began to form as soon as the boat was in; mothers, children, occasionally a fisherman, and Melissa Savage waited outside the locked post office until the truck arrived, the bags of mail were unloaded, and inside the mail was sorted. It was a conversational, patient line, strung out along the sidewalk past the drugstore; the children ate dripping ice-cream pops, and the women leaned their bare arms against the wall and talked together in the sun. Only Melissa Savage stood ramrod straight, fidgeting with the rings on her fingers. And when the post office door was unlocked and the line shortened and shortened as the mail was handed out, Melissa Savage moved forward and opened her bag. Her mail was handed her and she popped it in the bag, shut it, and strode outside. Her bag was long and woven and striped, perhaps

Mexican, and her heavy eyelids were creased with lines though she was only thirty years old.

Summer people, strange as they were, and with strange eating habits—asking for avocados in the grocery store, or kidneys—were humored and accepted. The lobstermen brought them crabs from the traps and the townswomen did their laundry. For the most part the summer people were families, or old married people with plenty of money who bought shapeless farmhouses and wore sneakers. But Melissa Savage lived alone. She had come in May and drove an old jeep station wagon cautiously through town; she had rented 'Lishe Young's house on Seal Point which was up for sale since the old man died. Whenever she came to town she wore the same sweater and skirt and sandals, though people who had seen her around 'Lishe's house saw her in pale-blue pants and a sleeveless jersey, and no shoes. With the vocabulary that the islanders had picked up from the city people, they had learned to call her bohemian.

She was friendly enough. She stood in the grocery store after paying for her food and spoke a minute with Mrs. Ames, who ran the store. In the paper store she discussed the news with Amos Geary and while she talked glanced through her copy of *The New York Times,* which she ordered special from the mainland, in case there was anything interesting to tell him that didn't make the Maine papers. Sometimes she even said "It was ninety-eight degrees in New York on Tuesday," though Amos was not interested in New York's weather, especially as this was Thursday; New York papers came two days late. She often stopped on the street to chat with someone she had met in a store; and she was direct and cheerful, spoke to children as though they were grown-ups like herself, and took time out to have a little gab with old Tinker Arey, who positioned himself in front of the firehouse on a cane chair, moving himself to keep up with the shade. She seemed to have a special affection for Tinker, though he was a mad old man, but harmless. Everyone who became her acquaintance called her Melissa to her face, for she was young and frank and had no fancy airs; but when they talked about her, they referred to her as Melissa Savage. And they often talked about her.

But one day her letter must have come; or else something in the New York paper pleased her. At any rate, between the post office and the paper store together, a foreign event changed her expression. Holding her mail in her hand, and with the *Times* under her arm, she crossed the street to the edge of the harbor where she read a few letters and looked up something in the paper. She re-crossed Main Street, her felt hat in one hand and her two dark eyes shining like horse chestnuts. You couldn't miss such an expression in the eyes of someone who usually seemed to be looking at you through the folds of a curtain. She stood in front of Tinker Arey, bending forward at him, for he was a bit deaf, her hair swinging over her cheeks, and she spoke in a precise happy voice that carried across the street. "Isn't it a beautiful day, Mr. Arey?" "Can't complain," Tinker replied; he was startled to see Melissa Savage with her hair free of her hat leaning so close over him he could whiff a little perfume smell or the smell of shampooed hair; she usually stood back under that foolish hat and didn't speak up loud enough for him to hear. Melissa straightened up with a smile and crossed the street directly toward Mrs. Ames, who was coming out of the post office opening the new Sears Roebuck catalog.

"Mrs. Ames, how would your daughter like to work for me?" Melissa asked. She stood with the sun full on her face, which was tanned and high in the cheekbones, lanky even, with heavy-lidded eyes and a mouth that turned down at the corners as though ravaged. Mrs. Ames studied this face while pretending she had not understood the question; it was one thing to talk to Melissa in the store, quite another to entrust Beatie to her.

"What's that?" Mrs. Ames asked.

"I was wondering if Beatie would like to work for me. You see I have a child coming to visit and I'd like someone—you know, a young girl—I'd like a young girl, just in the afternoon so I could be a little free. I'm not used to children, not all day long."

During this little speech Mrs. Ames went on studying the tanned lean face. Melissa was a kind enough girl, very polite, perhaps she would encourage Beatie to go off to college in two years. Beatie was a bright girl, all her teachers said so, but she had no ambitions and was too stuck on that Webster boy, a lazy, stupid fellow who tinkered with old cars. Well, why not let Beatie go to Melissa? It wouldn't do for Beatie to become too friendly, Melissa was an odd girl, a bohemian, but she might advise Beatie about colleges.

"I'll ask her tonight, Melissa; she's off swimming today. But I'm sure she's good with a child, she's done some baby-sitting. She's very quick to think up a game. Is this a boy or a girl?"

"A little boy, Greg. He's eight now. I'm sure she wouldn't have any trouble with him, he's well-behaved and very sweet. He's very sweet."

"I'm sure he is. I'll have Beatie call you tonight. She'll be tickled to death."

The two women smiled and separated. Mrs. Ames was wondering why a family would send off their little boy by himself to a girl living alone in the country. And Melissa was driving her jeep through town too fast, with all the windows down, and she had put her hat on again. But it was pushed back now so that it didn't dip down and shadow her face. And altogether it was clear in town that whatever Melissa Savage had been waiting for had come.

Many people saw the little boy arrive on the boat. As the passengers, islanders who had gone ashore for two days and a few summer visitors, came along the gang-plank, this little fellow came with them, by himself, carrying a small leather suitcase with two buckles on it. Melissa was standing right at the end of the plank, smiling, and the boy smiled cautiously back. He put down his suitcase and put up his arms, and she gripped him with her hands across his back and lifted him off the ground in a hug. He was a straight, frail, dark-haired child with a pale face, and feet that turned in slightly as he walked. He had very light eyes, like a fish's, that looked odd under his dark bangs. A weak sad city child with sharp little elbows and a pinched mouth. Poor waif, they were thinking, a proper companion for Melissa. She and the boy got into the jeep and drove off, and Beatie, who was standing with a group of friends to watch the boat come in, ran off to the grocery store to tell her mother she had seen the boy she was to take care of and thought him very puny.

The next day Beatie bicycled home from 'Lishe Young's house after her first day's work for Melissa. She pedaled furiously along the dirt road, little whorls of dust rising from her tires. The road ran between trees and was hot and windless. She pushed her hair back from her sweating forehead but pedaled faster to get home and tell her fa-

ther everything she'd learned. No one else had properly
visited Melissa, no one knew what she did with her day,
nor what had come in the trunks she had brought from
the city. But Beatie knew. Beatie knew and scorned, or
Beatie knew and admired. And the little boy was not
stuffy and citified, though he looked it. He was just serious. But very quick, and the first day out had put color in
his cheeks. He said his daddy wrote plays and had just
been sent off to France to see one produced over there. But
the craziest thing of all was that Greg called Melissa
Mommy. And though Melissa was very affectionate with
him, sometimes when he called her Mommy she smiled a
quizzical smile over the top of his head. And later, outdoors, when Beatie had questioned him, Greg said: "She's
not my mother but she lived with us for a while and I call
her my mother." "Where is your mother?" "I don't know,
I never see her." The bicycle tires ran off the dirt onto the
hardtop road near town and Beatie, passing houses now,
slowed down. For maybe her father would not like this
arrangement; there was something peculiar about Melissa
being Greg's mother but not his mother. Maybe her father wouldn't let her work for Melissa if he knew the
story—whatever the story was. She would keep her mouth
shut. She would not even tell that the trunks had only contained books, and that Melissa wrote something. Beatie
had seen pages and pages of handwritten papers on a
large table in the living room. Though she was not sure
herself whether it was foolish or admirable to write, she
was sure what her father would think. There had been a
painter who spent the summer in town and her father had
no end of things to say about him. She would tell him
nothing, she would not go directly home. A brittle liking
for Melissa had turned up that day, seeing her ob-

scured eyes over Greg's head; she would protect that. Beatie, deciding not to tell her father anything, swung off on a side road and pedaled at her own pace, aimlessly.

Beatie worked for weeks at Melissa's. She arrived in the early afternoon, usually when Greg and Melissa were finishing lunch. Beatie played with Greg for a few hours outdoors and when they came back in to have milk and cookies in the kitchen Melissa was still at the table in the living room and did not come in to see how they were. But they were always fine. Beatie liked Greg, Greg liked Beatie. He made up games which she ashamedly enjoyed acting out. First they sat in the field and Greg told her the story, he told it in detail, and then they got up and went into the characters. If she slipped in the role, he corrected her: "A general would never say that," or: "Italians don't eat hot dogs." And he was not rough like the boys in town. Sometimes at the end of the game (only he called them plays) he came up to her and put up his arms; his face, getting tanned now, moving cautiously upward; she bent to receive his kiss though his arms bumped her ears: he did not quite dare complete the hug. She liked this funny little boy whose pinched face took on a tan like a coat of varnish; for under the color he retained the drawn frail quality of someone whose bones lie close under the skin. The color seemed unnatural and she could see the vein beating in his neck.

At first Beatie asked him about his family. "Why did you come all alone on the boat?"

"Daddy put me on in Rockhaven. He drove me from New York."

"Why didn't he come over too? He's your mother's friend, ain't he?"

The boy turned his light eyes aside vaguely. "They had a fight."

"A fight?"

"Yes. Daddy doesn't love Mommy like I do. I heard him tell her so. She's not really my mother."

"You told me that. Don't you know your real mother?"

"No. But I know she's crazy."

"Crazy? What do you mean, crazy?"

"Mommy told Daddy I have to come visit her sometimes because I don't have a real mother." He suddenly looked at Beatie with his pale washed-out eyes. "I think she's in a hospital. For crazy people. They have that kind of hospital, don't they?"

"I guess they do," she said uneasily.

"Well that's where she is. And Mommy lived with us, that's why I call her my mother but she won't live with us any more."

"How do you know?"

"Daddy threw her out."

"He threw her *out*?"

"He told her to get out and she left, in the middle of the night. I heard everything."

They were sitting in a field; below them the high tide swayed between rocks. Greg lifted his eyes out to sea. "What's over there?"

"Portugal."

A round tear, like an abscess, formed under his lid. "Don't talk to me any more," he said. "I don't want to tell secrets."

Poor waif, Beatie's mother said. One day Melissa had driven Beatie and Greg into town so he could see it. Beatie took him to the grocery store to meet her mother. Mrs. Ames gave him a kiss, seeing him so thin and peaked;

he took a step backwards and looked at her dimly. "Aren't you having a grand summer though," she piped. "How do you like living on an island?" "New York's an island too." "So it is. But not like this one, is it now? Wouldn't you like to come back next summer?" "If Mommy buys the house I will." Mrs. Ames gave Beatie a quick look. Poor waif she said that night. Is Melissa Savage really his mother? And she never let on it was her child. I always said she was some odd, a bohemian, you know, Beatie, bringing a poor child like that into the world, and no father, God knows who takes care of him the rest of the year, and she's not much of a mother to look at. Well I'm some glad you're there every day, poor child he takes the heart.

Beatie did not tell her that Melissa was not the mother. The real story as she understood it was so much worse. Bitter bitter in what way she did not know, nor for whom it was bitter. But she suspected it was for Melissa Savage.

Beatie was a girl not at home with herself. When her mother said she had no ambition, she did not know where her daughter chose to place that ambition. Beatie sat in her bedroom with her chin on the sill staring between the steep roofs over the harbor to a wide Atlantic. Portugal. A man who did not stink of fish or grease. Wine. Last summer she had done baby-sitting for a summer family, and when they came home they opened a bottle of red wine and they all had a glass together; it stung her tongue, was sweet and sour like rotten raspberries, the glass stood curved and full of wine on a slender stem with a round flat base through which she saw, distorted, her fingers underneath. In Portugal they drank wine. All her life her father and the other lobstermen had told her that directly across the ocean was Portugal. It had marked the end of water all her life. And she had lived her life surrounded by water, stranded by it on a small island where the men stank. Ned Webster who took her out in his car stank of oil and fish bait. He talked about how he would someday own a garage on the mainland so he could go dancing on Saturdays and go to the movies every night. She felt a sickening recognition of that life, that she would sit beside him in the movies, smelling him again, smelling the grease, then he would drink whiskey and not let her have any so that he would stink of whiskey; just like her father who wouldn't let her mother have a drink, while she, Beatie, had had wine. In Portugal she would drink wine. The other end of this water which damned her to Ned Webster was Portugal.

No one gave Beatie a book to read. There was no music except popular music from the Portland station. Movies came once a week in summer and they were deadly, she knew, about the rich and lazy, or about murder and cowboys. But dreams survive on very little. And when Beatie sat with Greg in the field she dreamt. He was not like the island boys, tough strong-boned little boys who punched and guffawed like small versions of Ned Webster. Greg's cheekbones were fragile as shells under the skin, his eyes were all watered out, his thin little mouth was drawn like a zipper above the solemn fix of his chin. Beatie was sixteen, and sixteen-year-old girls rarely dream of having a child; but in her dreaming there was the beginning of the dream to have a child, and that child must be a child like Greg, and that child Ned Webster would never give her.

And so she protected Melissa's secret, because Melissa

was a woman. Though she had no idea what the secret was. *She lived with us for a while and I call her my mother. He told her to get out and she left, in the middle of the night. Daddy doesn't love Mommy like I do.* And everyone in town noticed that Melissa picked up her mail indifferently now. She no longer stood in line with that fixed ramrod look about her. She had gotten what she was waiting for, and all it was was a waif of a child, her own they said, though she didn't seem to spare any love for it. She must have looked forward to his coming, the way she used to grab those letters. He's all she has, waif though he is. But I always said she was queer in the head, not all there. Very pleasant she is, always was, but not all there.

Beatie took courage. She told Greg to sit there in the kitchen and drink his milk, and she went into the living room. Melissa was sitting straight up in the chair, her back to Beatie. She sat still, but for her hands twisting in front of her, turning the rings on her fingers.

"Melissa," Beatie said with a rough throat.

Melissa's head swung profile. "What is it, Beatie?"

"I just . . . I was wondering . . . you write, don't you?"

Melissa turned in the chair and set her dark flat eyes on Beatie's face. The awkward girl, the abstracted woman took a short thoughtful look at each other. "Yes," said Melissa abruptly.

"Did you go to college?"

Melissa stirred in her chair, put her hand back through her hair, and then her eyes went gentle, seemed to sink back in her face under their heavy lids. And Beatie, to avoid those eyes, shifted her own, and saw on the table a paper dated July 29: Greg's socks Greg's socks—written at least fifty times.

"Sit down, Beatie. Here, sit over here."

She moved two books out of a chair and Beatie sat down and leaned her arms on her rough knees, her head lowered and determined. She had seen the eyes go gentle.

"Your mother wants you to go to college, doesn't she?"

"Yes. But I don't want to go. I'd have to go to the University of Maine. I'm . . . oh I'm sick of boys from Maine. They all stink, they stink of fish and things. I want to go away. Do the boys in New York stink like that?"

"No, but they have other troubles. Nobody likes their home-grown men."

"What do you mean?"

"*I*'m sick of what men in New York stink of, brains and talent and egotism." She laughed suddenly. "So I find your fish-smelling men rather nice. I find them rather nice. But look, we're talking about you. There are other universities besides Maine."

"I'd never get in. I wouldn't know where to start. I . . . I have no clothes. My mother takes me to Rockhaven shopping in the fall, for school, but I know what they wear in the cities, I look at the magazines sometimes in Amos's. I couldn't go anywhere. I'm not fit."

"That's nonsense. You're bright. You're bright. Your mother told me you do well in school. I met Mr. Fairweather in town, he said you're the best student in history."

"History! I want to go . . . to Portugal. I want to drink wine. I had some once, at the Spitzers'."

"Well look, that's easy. That's easy."

Melissa opened a cupboard, took out a bottle and two

173

glasses. She poured the glasses full and gave one to Beatie who held it shakily. It was in her hand but she was still on this side of the Atlantic. With Ned tonight, thrashing with her in his car. The sweet stinging taste revolted her; this much she could get, but no closer. Melissa held her glass without drinking and looked closely at the girl.

"Your name's Beatrice, isn't it?"

"Yes."

"That's a pretty name and you're a pretty girl. You're a pretty girl. You won't have any trouble." No one had ever called Beatie pretty, not even Ned, who said she had the roundest face this side of the moon. "You can't just go somewhere, like Portugal, that takes money, freedom, everything you haven't got. But you can go to college. You can go to college in New York. Then you hear of things, colleges in Europe you can transfer to, you'll make friends who want to travel together for the summer, so you'll go. It takes time. It takes time, these things you want." Melissa was leaning forward looking fixedly at Beatie. The pictures stood up before the girl's mind.

"Did you do that?"

"It can be done."

"I'll never be able to do it. I don't know anything. I've never been on a bus."

"You can learn to take a bus, to buy the kind of dresses they wear in the city. You can go to Europe. You can meet men who don't stink. It's not so hard once you start."

"How will I start? Even Greg knows how to take a bus."

This was the first time Beatie had ever talked about leaving Maine; talking made it seem impossible; dreaming was easy, impractical, and skipped over years. She sat forward, her arms on her scratched knees, knowing herself to be a lump of a girl with thick wild hair, still in high school, with awkward dreams that seemed bruised now; she was stuck, stuck, condemned to this rock surrounded by water at the other end of which her dream hovered, unseen, over the curve of the world; left to Ned Webster and his grabbing rough hands in the front seat of a car; but real, those hands, better than nothing, tempting. Melissa sat watching until Beatie raised her eyes, and this time the girl and the woman looked long at each other. There was a foggy look in Melissa's eyes; they seemed to draw at Beatie; they were enormous under their heavy lids, compelling; they were drawing a look into Beatie's which she felt and was afraid of. As though her own eyes had been pulled out of her head and been absorbed.

"Greg," Melissa said warmly. "You think Greg is better off because he can take a bus? Listen to me, Beatie, I'll help you. I'll help you."

Greg came into the room. "What are you talking about, Mommy?"

"We're talking about Beatie going to college. Maybe she'll come to New York."

"Come!" he said, with a flicker of a laugh. "We'll go to the zoo."

"You'd like Beatie to come to New York, wouldn't you, pumpkin?" Melissa said and put out her hands, pulled him up to her, and kissed his face, his eyes, his mouth, his cheeks, his neck. "I only had one thing to do today, Greg. I only had to fix your socks and I haven't done it. You remember I told you this morning I only had one thing to do?"

Greg stood under the kisses with his face lifted. For the only time Beatie saw Melissa with tears in her eyes and that was odd, for she was smiling.

And so there were weeks: sun: fog: rain. But often when Beatie and Greg were sitting in the kitchen Melissa called her in. They had a glass of sherry together, and sometimes Melissa looked that look that seemed to absorb Beatie's eyes. And often now Melissa came outdoors with Beatie and Greg and joined in their plays; or they walked along the shore looking for unbroken sea urchins. Summer was passing; the rose hips reddened on the bushes, the grass in fields was burnt yellow, and yellow islands floated on a darker sea. Melissa walked along barefoot and asked Beatie about lobsters, winter storms, if the coves iced over, about gulls and seals, and the names of wild plants. On foggy or raining days they all sat in the kitchen around the block of warmth from the stove. Beatie made them a pie, telling Melissa about the dough and the berries, and laughing because Melissa had never made a pie. In the process of these days Beatie learned the names of colleges in New York, the names of avenues, of Harlem, the Village, and the Battery. Melissa drew a map, on a napkin, of Manhattan like a ship with its bow in the Atlantic until Beatie could draw her own and line it with avenues and sections. And if Melissa went back into the living room, Beatie and Greg leaned on their elbows across the table from each other and whispered stories. At the end of the afternoon Beatie wheeled her bike into the road and swung on, coasted downhill through the field, and looked back once at the white house among the apple trees where her best hours were spent. She did not feel like Beatie; she felt unfamiliar. She no longer dreamed. The dream had become an ordeal, something to grapple with, like a bad conscience. It was coming closer like land in fog, darkening, impending. Almost it had a name.

It was a fine blue day, cloudless, with an east wind: a weather-breeder that would bring fog the next day. Hard to believe, under the blueness. Beatie and Greg were sitting above the rocks. Greg was telling her something, she listened but she was looking. And she saw with shock what she had never seen but had been there to see; she saw the lids above the eyes. She had been distracted by his pale eyes, so in contrast with the dark hair, mysteriously pale as though under water. Now she saw the lids, heavy lids though the eyes were large, and she had never seen such lids before. Only on Melissa. That was very odd. Odd and disturbing. It struck her there was something she knew but couldn't locate in her mind. It made bad sense.

Melissa Savage still came to town, of course. But not as often. She stopped on the street to talk to everyone, and in stores, just as she always had. But her hands, with their confusion of rings—you simply couldn't tell if one of them was a wedding ring—bunched together, gripping and bunching. And, talking to someone, she dragged one of those hands away from the other and set it on her companion's elbow in an urgent, gripping contact. With the penetrating often cruel judgment of people who do not trust strangers, the townspeople saw a change coming over her coincidental with their knowledge that she was the mother of the child. When she stopped to talk with someone there was now, perhaps had always been, a weird expression across her face, a devouring, devoured look. Only Tinker Arey still welcomed her little visit, and the two of them, the old man sitting, the woman bending over him, had long aimless conversations in the shade of the fire house. Deaf as a post, crazy as a coot, they thought him the best companion for Melissa Savage. And when she brought Greg into town with her, they looked with wondering pity; at this little fish gaping up at them. They pumped Beatie for gossip but she had none to give. Mrs. Ames was sorry she had allowed her daughter to work for Melissa; the girl had changed, spoke less, no longer joined her friends swimming, in fact spent more and more time at Melissa's and came home in a daze. Her round face seemed to have lengthened and hardened. She was becoming peculiar herself.

Beatie and Greg were sitting on the kitchen step.

"Will you ask Mommy to take us to town?"

"You ask her. I don't know where she is."

"She went down to the woods there. You go ask her, Beatie, I'm making a costume."

Beatie set off reluctantly, walking down through the field, took the path through the fringe of woods thick with young alders, and into the deep woods. Wind thrashed at the tops of spruces but was still near the ground: hot and still, and there was a faint marsh smell underfoot. It was like sinking in a well; the sounds, even the sound of sea on rock, rose above her, the air clamped itself on her mouth. The path fell apart in the woods, and the woods were tangled with moss, dead sunless trees were fallen over each other, and nothing gave a hint of a human having passed that way. Beatie stopped, wanting to go back up the hill to Greg, but she made her way along, dry branches against her bare dry arms and legs. One did not get lost in such small woods, she knew; nevertheless she lost direction; overhead the sky was obscurely blue, almost white with heat, no sun in sight. Beatie could not remember ever having been in the woods. She had walked along town roads to the quarries to swim, climbed along the shore near town, or walked in fields around friends' houses; but it was choking in the woods, airless, dead. It occurred to her to call. She raised a tiny voice: "Melissa," and clearing her throat tried again: "Melissa!" It projected no further than the meshed line of trees circling her. Beatie was lost now. She would walk till she came to something, a road, the shore. Trees pressed her; the air stuck in her throat. She pushed through branches; she would have cried, only she was afraid of giving out. Then there was daylight, sunlight, an opening, a field. In the middle of that field Melissa stood.

She stood with her hands over her ears and her elbows out, like someone shutting out sound. With her back to Beatie, she nevertheless displayed pleading. Her head was thrown back and she stood on her bare heels swayingly. Then she began to walk in a large slow circle. Beatie, grateful for a human, waited uneasily at the edge of the woods; wanted to run forward, saw in Melissa something to hold her back in a cringe.

Melissa, with her head back, passed once in her circle without seeing Beatie; the next time around, her eyes landed on the girl, who put out her chin. Melissa came up close and Beatie saw the corners of Melissa's mouth, which were always turned down, stretched away from her teeth. Thrusting her hands up against her cheekbones, she surveyed Beatie; the rings hung on her fingers as though she had grown skinny in the field.

"What are you doing here?"

"Greg wants to go to town."

"Then we'll go. Do you think I can't do something as simple as that when I'm like this?"

"What?"

But Melissa took Beatie's arms, grippingly. "Come back to the city with us, Beatie. You're better for Greg than I am. He's all muddled up, he's too soft. Come with us. I'm no mother for him."

"Are you his real mother?"

"Me? God yes, if you can call me real," she laughed. "Sane women get their children. Not me." She released Beatie and pressed her hands up against her cheeks again. "Listen, Beatie, do you understand?"

"Sort of."

"Come to the city. Come to the city with us, Beatie."

"Are you going to live with them again?"

"No that's true. I won't live with them."

"Greg doesn't think you're his real mother, you know."

"Doesn't he? That's what I mean. He's all muddled. He's all muddled. I spent half his childhood in the hospital, why should he think I'm his mother? Why am I talking to you? You stay here, have a sane life, stay where you belong, have lots of healthy children. Don't burst your brains protecting a soft boy like Greg. You have strong tough little babies. Only you love Greg, don't you."

"I guess I do."

"Let's go. What was I thinking? You can't come to the city with us. We're leaving tomorrow anyway. His father wants him back."

"Melissa! Melissa?"

The woman smiled, out of startled eyes as though she only then realized she had been speaking. Overhead a white sky glazed over them, and Melissa shook Beatie's arm once, dropping it swiftly. Together they went up through the woods, Melissa walking unerringly till they came to the path. They walked up through the field to the house. Greg ran down from the house with a false beard strapped to his chin. When he reached Melissa she snatched it off.

"You'll grow up soon enough, Greg," she said while he stood back alarmed. Then she laughed and laughed. "Here, put it back on. You look just right in it. Like a little midget. With your old eyes. Where did you get those old eyes? Aren't you a little boy, aren't you eight years old? How did you learn to look like an old man?"

Greg stood with the beard dangling from his neck on its string. Beatie burst into tears. It all made that bad sense. Greg like a small grown-up man whose beard had fallen off his chin. Melissa laughing and getting down on her knees in the grass hugging the boy around the waist while he turned his light eyes past her shoulder to sea. It was Beatie, crying, who took the beard off from around his neck and put it on her own face. Melissa kneeling in the grass Beatie weeping and striding up and down like a man barking orders to imaginary servants and swinging an imaginary cane Greg clapping his hands with joy; rescued, he shouted with laughter and ignoring his mother on her knees he ran ahead of Beatie screaming in delight with all his little teeth showing between the thin lips. Together they left Melissa kneeling, and she laughed, knelt laughing and calling: "You're both crazy. You're mad, the two of you." But they were out of earshot.

A NOTE ABOUT THE AUTHOR

Lucy Warner was born in 1940 in New York. She attended
Sarah Lawrence College, spent a year in Italy, and finished
her education at the State University of Iowa, where she was
a member of the Writer's Workshop. While she was still in
college she won an *Atlantic Monthly* "First" for the most
promising story by a writer not previously published. Miss
Warner has worked in bookstores in Iowa City and New
York City and has been an editorial assistant at *The New
York Review of Books*. Lately she has spent all her time writing and is living in Cambridge, Massachusetts.

A NOTE ON THE TYPE

This book was set on the Linotype in Baskerville. The punches for this face were cut under the supervision of George W. Jones, the eminent English printer and the designer of Granjon and Estienne. Linotype Baskerville is a facsimile cutting from type cast from the original matrices of a face designed by John Baskerville, a writing master of Birmingham, for his own private press. The original face was the forerunner of the "modern" group of type faces, known today as Scotch, Bodoni, etc. After his death in 1775, Baskerville's punches and matrices were sold in France and were used to produce the sumptuous Kehl edition of Voltaire's works.

This book was composed, printed, and bound by The Colonial Press Inc., Clinton, Massachusetts.

Typography and binding design by Golda Fishbein.